Dance Me Outside

Dance Me Outside
W. P. Kinsella

Toronto: Reference Press 1987

This Large Print edition is available through
arrangement with Oberon Press, Ottawa.

Surprise (1972) by Jeremy Smith, from the collection of
Gerry Clark, is reproduced on the front of the jacket
with the permission of Jeremy Smith
and the Mira Godard Gallery.

Published in Canada by Reference Press
Box 1141, Station F,
Toronto, Ontario M4Y 2T8

Set in 16 point Sabon Bold
Printed and bound in Canada

Canadian Cataloguing in Publication Data

Kinsella, W.P.

Dance me outside

ISBN 0-919981-13-5

1. Large type books.   I. Title.

PS8571.I57D36 1987   C813'.54   C86-093745-3
PR9199.3.K59D36 1987

Illianna Comes Home

My name is Silas Ermineskin. I am eighteen years old. Me and Frank Fence-post and a couple of other guys are taking a course that the government offers on how to be mechanics. I fix things pretty good and our instructor, Mr. Nichols, say he think he can get me an apprentice job with a tractor company in Wetaskiwin when I finish.

One part of the course I don't like is that I got to write an essay. I'm lucky I can write. Frank Fence-post can write most of his name, but he is faking everything else since the course started. Mr. Nichols say I got a funny sense of humour, so I should just write about the funniest thing that ever happened to me.

I been thinking about that, and I think the funniest thing that ever happened to me was when my sister Illianna came home to the reserve with her white man husband.

Illianna she smart. She stayed at school until grade eight and then went all the way to Calgary to work. She worked too. Waited tables at the New Zenith Cafe and she don't drink and do bad things like Suzie Calf-robe and some of the other girls who go to the city. Illianna she pretty, and she proud she pretty. She say to me in one of her letters she not going to do nothing to spoil herself, like drink and fight.

Eathen Firstrider he sure is mad when she up and goes away, because he been her boy-friend ever since she was twelve, and he figure they would get married. Eathen he won $50 in the calf-roping contest at the Ponoka Stampede last summer. When he do, he buy a record of Buffy St. Marie, even though he ain't got no record player, because he say she look like Illi-anna. He got the record picture on the wall of his cabin. He still figures that he gonna marry with Illianna some day.

Then Illianna writes home that she married with a white man. Mrs. Robert McGregor McVey is what we should call her now. Her husband is a businessman. He's old too, 25, and even been for one year to the university some-where. Illianna she don't work no more and they got an apartment in one of the big build-ings in Calgary.

Ma, she has bad feelings that our Illianna married with a white man. But she not half as mad as Eathen Firstrider when I tell him. Eathen, he polishes the big blade of his hunting knife on his jeans and talks about taking scalps. Frank Fence-post, he laugh and say, "We don't do that no more."

"It's time we started again," says Eathen. Then he throws the knife right through the one-by-four side of the kindling box. Eathen he's already twenty and all us guys look up to him. He rides in the rodeos and knows all about girls and cars. Two years ago he was outrider on the chuckwagon races at the Calgary Stampede. He spent $25 of his wages on a white girl down at the Queen's Hotel, and she taught him all kinds of things that he wasn't too sure about. When he got back he told us guys about it for two hours and how he was gonna do all these things with Illianna. And he weren't lying to us. He don't know, but me and Frank and Charlie Fence-post was hanging off the roof of the cabin looking in the window.

Eathen sure figured that he was going to marry Illianna, but it wasn't long until she went away to Calgary. Eathen still figures all them things he taught her made her able to catch a white man, and he gets mad every time he think about it. But I bet Illianna being tall and slim and pretty helped some too.

Anyway, Illianna was married a year when she say in a letter she coming home for a long weekend with her white man husband.

They pull into the yard in a new car, one with chrome wheels and white and blue racing stripes. A car so big and new that it looks like it belong to a finance man.

The car stops and the kids come creeping out from behind the cabins like the deer do sometimes when they think there is no-one around. The kids walk with their necks out and like they haven't got any toes. Eathen Firstrider is standing cross-legged against the wall of his cabin, smoking a roll-yer-own that is about as long and thin as he is.

If Illianna wasn't my sister, I wouldn't have known her. She let her hair grow real long and she be wearing a white coat, a white suit, and white boots. I think while I'm walking up to her that Illianna, she going to be a white woman one way or another.

Then her husband, he get out, and he look like one of them pictures out of the Eaton's catalogue. He got a hat with a funny little brim, an overcoat, and a suit and tie. He got shiny black shoes with toe rubbers too.

He shake hands with me, and Ma too. Ma ignores him, and she don't speak so much on Illianna. Ma's wearing her good speckled dress and her purple kerchief. She looks in the back of the car, not walking over to it but just by rolling her eyes. Then she looks hard on Illianna's tummy and say, "Where your babies?"

"Ma," Illianna say, giving her a real harsh look.

"Well, where your babies?"

"We haven't got any babies."

"How come? You been married most a

year. When I been married a year I had you and Joseph already, and Silas in my stomach."

"Really Ma. We just don't want children yet." Illianna, by her voice lets Ma know she wishes she would shut up. Ma just nods knowingly and continues right on.

"What's with don't want? You get a good man you get lots of babies. What's wrong with him?" She nods toward McVey who has been standing like he frozen, one hand stuck out in front like maybe he going to shake hands on someone else. About this time Eathen Firstrider strolls across the yard, walking very slow.

"Hello Illianna," he says. Then he say some very personal things to her in our language. Now I know why Ma and Eathen have been holding council in our cabin for the last three days. That white man, he'd take his hand back quick if he knew what Eathen was saying. Illianna's cheeks get bright pink and she looks sharp on her McVey, but he is not interested in Eathen.

McVey has moved in on Ma, and he is trying to make himself useful by explaining his financial position and telling her that it will be two more years before they can afford babies. He assures Ma that Illianna and him will have kids when they want them, only I'm sure I hear him say something about papooses. Ma she just look blank and roll her eyes like when she have too much moonshine. Illianna she got one hand on McVey's sleeve kind of pulling him back, but she listening too, only to Eathen Firstrider, who say things that make everyone blush, except McVey, who don't know anyone but him is talking.

When McVey stops for breath, Ma, she just goes on from where she left off before.

"Louis Coyote, he blind," she say, "he lost his leg when the tractor run over him, but he still makes babies. Edith Coyote pop any day now with their fifteenth."

McVey he just kind of shake his head, then he explain things to Ma again. Only this time he tells it like he was talking to a little kid. When he is finished Ma speaks in our language to Illianna.

"What's she say?" McVey asks Illianna.

"She wants me to tell her what you said."

"But you said she understands English... "

Ma interrupted him again to speak to Illianna.

"She says she only understands English when an Indian speaks it," says Illianna.

"That's impossible," says McVey, who is about a foot shorter than Eathen, even with his fancy hat on.

"I'm sorry, Bob," Illianna says, "let's go inside. I'll have a talk with Ma later."

Then she gives Eathen a funny smile, and me the same, like she was saying the thing for her to do was get into the fancy car and drive back to the city. Instead, we all go into the cabin where Ma is mumbling in our language about, "Money don't have nothing to do with make babies."

"I'll bring in your suitcase," I say to McVey.

He looks hard on Illianna, but she smiles on me.

"That would be very nice, Silas," she says.

McVey gives me the keys to his car, but very slowly like it is part of his hand he is passing to me.

"You be careful you don't scratch nothing, Si," he says to me. Si, I ain't never been called Si in my whole life.

There must be fifteen kids gathered around the car with their faces pressed against the windows. They are just looking at the white upholstery and touching the shiny paint. Frank Fence-post is there running the aerial up and down. I get the suitcase out of the back seat and one of the younger kids lugs it into the cabin. My girlfriend, Sadie One-wound has arrived.

"Boy, that's some big car," she says, "Will you buy us one like this when you get a job?"

"First pay cheque," I promise.

"Can I sit in it, Silas?"

"Well, I don't know." But Frank already has the door open and about a dozen kids are climbing in the back. I get behind the wheel, just to keep Frank from sitting there, and Sadie crawls over me and squeezes in next to

Frank. Margaret Standing-at-the-door has just crawled through the passenger window and is sitting on Frank's lap.

"Start it up," yells Sadie, and the kids in the back cheer. I figure it won't do no harm to start the motor, so I give the key a turn and boy do it ever start fast.

Up to this time I ain't drove so much. I used to sit in the One-wound's Studebaker with no wheels and shift gears until the finance men came and towed it away.

About ten seconds after I start the car my brother-in-law charges out of the cabin, and he's coming for me with a not nice look on his face.

"Get going," yells Frank. Then he pulls the gear-shift into drive, reaches over and stomps my foot on the gas pedal so hard that the car nearly stands on its hind legs. The car sprays dirt and gravel and from the terrible yell I hear, I guess that McVey was behind the car. We shoot straight ahead, miss the corner of One-wound's cabin by only a little bit, and lose Charlie Fence-post who was too late to get in the car, but was sitting on the hood.

"Steer," yells Sadie above everyone else. But I just watch what is happening, which is when we drive over part of an old land disc, a tire goes bang and we swing to the left and straight into the slough behind Wolfchild's cabin. V-room, v-room, the car goes, and shoots mud

12

and water back a long way, which is far enough to spray McVey and Charlie Fence-post who are coming after us. The kids in the back are all cheering. Sadie One-wound hugs my arm, and the car still goes v-room, v-room.

McVey runs into the water, opens the door and pulls out the keys. He uses cuss words on me that I never heard before, so I guess there are still things we can learn from the white man. Me and Frank are busy saying how we'll get Louis Coyote's pickup and pull the car right out. McVey is busy clearing the kids out of the back of the car and telling me to shut to hell up, and he'll call the AMA, whatever that is. I hope it ain't nothing to do with the RCMP.

It turns out that the AMA is the tow truck up at Wetaskiwin, which is about eleven miles away. McVey he say he don't need no help from us, but after he walks all the way to Hobbema Crossing to use the phone at the service station, with us and the little kids walking a respectable distance behind him, it seems that the tow truck won't come out to the reserve for nobody no matter how white he is. So we all go and get Louis Coyote's pickup and with McVey direct-ing, pull the car out and change the tire. Illianna is really mad with us, because mainly of McVey's suit which she say cost $200, and the fact, she says, that he catches cold so easy.

We all try to talk soft on him after that. I take him for a walk around the reserve, along the way we pick up the Fence-post boys and a few others. I show him my collection of car parts. Frank, he talks lots about how we strip down cars when we know the finance men coming to take them away, and how we changed plates and painted Louis Coyote's pickup so that even the finance men don't know it no more.

"It been most a year since anyone been looking for that truck," says Frank, and tells about how when we hear the finance men is coming we quick tear up the culvert by the slough so they got to walk instead of drive around the reserve.

"I am employed by a finance company," says my brother-in-law.

"Hey, partner, I been lying to you," says Frank thinking real fast.

McVey gives us a talk like they do down to the technical school, and he use the same voice he used on Ma a while ago. He tells us how it's not nice to strip down cars and trucks and how other people have to pay for it when we do things like that, and how if we'd only pay our bills there wouldn't be no trouble.

Frank, he say it sure is nice for them other people to pay and all, because he always been worried that the RCMP come around looking for something else but moonshine. Brother Bob he just shake his head and kick little rocks with his toe rubbers.

"You think we should let him get away?" Frank says to me in our language. "You can bet the finance man's gonna come back after Louis' pickup, and maybe even the RCMP after our car parts."

"We could drown him over in Muskrat Lake," says Charlie Fence-post. "Illianna, she don't miss him after a couple of days, and I bet nobody else would."

"Or we could just sort of lose him, leave him out in the dark for Eathen Firstrider to find," says Frank.

"I have a better idea," I say. "We don't do nothing to him. Ma and Mad Etta and Eathen, they got something planned. Better we shouldn't do nothing to upset it."

"What are you guys talking about," says McVey.

"We sure do like your little rubber shoes, partner," Frank tells him.

It sure is bad that McVey should be a finance man. This makes him to us like the cavalry must have been to the old time Indian. He is also like magpie, whenever his mouth open bad sounds come out. When I tell him my girlfriend Sadie One-wound has fifteen brothers and sisters, McVey, he say with a laugh, "No wonder they call you guys fucking Indians." No-one laugh and McVey he sure wish he is back in the big city.

Ma been holding council with Mad Etta

15

over to her cabin. Mad Etta is sort of our medicine man. She is so big she got a tree-trunk chair over at her cabin, because ordinary chairs crack up when she sits on them. I've seen them bulldog smaller steers at the rodeos. Everyone know that over at the Alice Hotel in Wetaskiwin, they got two chairs wired together and braced with two-by-fours so Mad Etta can drink beer and not bust up the furniture.

It is next morning before we find out what Ma and Mad Etta are planning. The night before, we give Illianna and her husband the other bed in the cabin, so me and the kids sleep on the floor. I lie awake and listen while Illianna teases McVey in a nice way, about they should try to make a baby.

"Good God, no," says McVey, "why there must be ten other people all around us."

Illianna laugh her pretty laugh and say that they won't hear nothing that they haven't heard before. And I bet she thinking of the fun she used to have with Eathen Firstrider back when she lived here and that used to be her bed.

I can tell by the way the cabin creaks that Frank Fence-post is on the roof, hanging over the edge and looking in on Illianna and her white man. He may as well go to sleep like I do.

At breakfast, Ma talks away in our language.

"You got to get him out for the evening, me and Mad Etta and somebody else we got a nice surprise for Illianna." By her tone of voice nobody would know she wasn't talking about the porridge she is stirring up. The 'him' she talks about is of course McVey, but she refer to him in our language as, "he who has no balls."

Illianna lights into Ma after that, and McVey must figure nobody speaks English no more as he sits polishing his spoon and knife on his tie.

Ma, she don't back away one bit. What she says to Illianna is pretty hard to make into English but it amount to, "You may love your white man for the fancy things he can give you but you still got hot pants for Eathen First-rider."

Illianna, she laugh and throw up her hands. Then she say to McVey in English, "You wear your warm coat today. You know how easy you take cold."

After breakfast, I say to McVey, "Brother Bob, we is really sorry about what we do to the car and for all the trouble we cause. We want you should enjoy your visit here, so tonight me and Frank and some of the boys, we make party for you. Show you good time. We going to make you an honourary Indian, just like when the Premier come down here to get us to vote for him."

You had better believe that I had to do some tall talking to get the boys to agree to that. I say, "Look, we make him a blood brother, he won't go sending the other finance men snooping around here and he don't send the RCMP after our car parts. It a lot better than killing him. Besides, I think he would like to be nice to us but he don't know how."

"We should drown him in Muskrat Lake," says Frank Fence-post.

McVey look at me up and down like maybe I want to borrow money from him. Then he say he guesses it would be okay we have the party. We say fine, and start to make plans that we take him to the ceremonial clearing which is way back in the hills a half mile, and which we just decide is going to be ceremonial clearing.

We send Frank Fence-post down to the Chief's cabin to borrow the ceremonial war bonnet, the same one we tie on the Premier and some French hockey player who claimed he was a quarter Assinoboine. But word travels fast on the reserve and the Chief he say among other things no white finance man ever going to wear the tribal war bonnet. So instead of war bonnet, Frank he come back with a five gallon cream-can full of dandelion wine that he borrow without asking.

Most of the day McVey he stay pretty close to Illianna and to his fancy car. About supper time, me and the boys go over to Mad Etta's. She been three days boiling up some strong medicine for Eathen Firstrider. Mad Etta she make the medicine out of tiger lilies, paintbrush, pig bristles, and many things that only she know about. It smell so strong that it hurt my nose from outside the cabin. We have to make fun on Eathen so that he brave to go in. The medicine be boiling on the back of the stove in an open pan, and it look like an oil change down at the Texaco garage.

Eathen is now not nearly so brave or so tall as he has been.

"How I going to drink pig bristles?" he wants to know.

"You drink," say Mad Etta, "or Etta sit on you and make you drink."

We all make some more fun on Eathen so he has to drink or look like he afraid. So he drink.

"You make many babies now," says Mad Etta. "Anybody you lie down with have many babies, even Etta." Then she laugh and laugh, shaking on her tree-trunk chair.

"Etta could have babies and nobody would know," she say, and laugh and laugh, patting her five-flour-sack dress.

My girlfriend, Sadie One-wound stop me on the way home from Mad Etta's and wants to know who pulled most of the feathers out of the turkey that her father keeps in a pen behind their house. I don't know.

But I find out when all us guys get to the clearing about nine that evening. Frank and Charlie got a good fire going and they already been sampling the wine that they borrowed.

Frank, he got a long piece of paper with turkey feathers glued down each side, and he fasten this on Brother Bob's head as soon as we get there.

"We is sorry we can't get the tribal war bonnet from the Chief," he say, "but this we make ourselves."

"It's very nice," Brother Bob say, but he look around funny like maybe he wish he have some other finance men there to keep him company.

Frank gets a big water dipper full of wine and gives it to McVey.

"That don't taste like wine," my brother-in-law say, "it's too sweet."

"Plenty honey in it," says Frank.

"It's the frogs that give it the sweet taste," says Charlie.

Brother Bob kind of choke a little, but then he see that we are just making fun on him. McVey goes to put down the dipper, but Frank lifts his arm back up.

"You gonna be Indian, you drink like Indian."

So Brother Bob finishes the dipper and Frank fills it again.

"I didn't mean to say it wasn't good," he say, and he smile on us for the first time since he come home with Illianna.

Illianna make me promise to look after McVey and see that he don't catch no cold. I figure that plenty of wine keep him warm and also make him nice to know. We all know that home-made wine kick harder than bucking horse. But McVey he don't know that.

After a while we all have lots of wine and we make noises and dance around the way we think a white man would expect us to. Then we put our hands on his hands and name him Robert Fire-chief our blood brother. Fire-chief is a name that Frank got from down at Hobbema Texaco garage.

Like I promised Illianna, I try to look after our new Indian, but after the wine starts him to glow, he runs around making what he thinks are war whoops, and singing "One Little, Two Little, Three Little Indians," and stomping around in a circle like a movie Indian.

McVey thinks that the name Fire-chief makes him a chief. So he lead up whooping around the clearing and then down the trail a ways. He is yelling something about Tonto and silver bullets. What he don't know is that we coming to a pretty deep creek. I remember what I promise Illianna and am just about to tell him watch out, when a little by himself and with a little help from Frank Fence-post he falls head first into the water. He come up looking like a calf in a mud hole.

He is one wet Indian. We herd him back to Wolfchild's cabin which is the closest one to where we are. He is sneezing already, and boy do I know Illianna is going to be mad on me. We set McVey on the floor in front of the stove which Frank and me is filling with cut pine. Then we dig up an old pair of Eddy Wolfchild's jeans and a shirt that belong to his sister.

"That's mighty white of you guys," say my brother-in-law.

While we are wiping off the mud and trying to warm up our new Indian, Charlie Fence-post comes running back from our cabin where he has gone to check on how Eathen is doing. He pull me off to one side.

"Eathen over there all right," he say, "but it no wonder she ain't got no babies. Even I know they don't get no babies from what they doing to each other."

"Give Eathen time," I say, "he got to do first all the tricks that white girl in Calgary showed him. Eathen he know how babies made, but with Mad Etta's medicine in him, he get babies any way he do it."

Edith Wolfchild comes home while we all sitting around. She look at Brother Bob shivering on the floor.

"You cold, huh?" she say to him, and then cuddles up close.

Frank Fence-post he makes a bad face, but I say pointing at McVey, "He blood brother now, if Edith likes him that's her business."

I don't think Edith so much likes McVey as she don't like Illianna, which is a long time story, so guess she figures to get even on Illianna for whatever wrong she done her. Edith puts her fat little arms around McVey and kisses him lots. He come to life and touch her back some. She lead him over to the bed and start taking off the clothes that we just put on him.

"Go away, you guys," she says to us, but we don't.

They get under the covers. Edith is do a lot of moving around, but I think I can hear Brother Bob's teeth still chattering. Before long Edith gets out of bed and starts putting on her clothes. McVey, looking very sick, wraps a blanket around himself and sits on the oven door. The cabin gets a little warm by now.

Eathen comes running into the cabin. He is about a foot taller than he was over at Mad Etta's, so I know without asking that all has gone pretty good over at our place. He smile a lot on Robert Fire-chief.

"We are blood brothers, now," he tells him a few times.

Eathen sure feels big to tell him this. Fire-chief just sits stupid on the oven door. He has eyes like a dead owl and burps a lot.

Next morning, McVey is very pale, even for a white man, very quiet and look some smaller than when he come. He also has a cold for which Illianna is very mad on me and the boys. Me and the Fence-post boys say good-bye to him in his Indian name and he seem some pleased.

"Fire-water plenty bad," he say, and try to laugh, but we can see it hurt his head to do that. Eathen saunters by and smile on Illianna. He tells Illianna personal things again.

"Next time you come bring lots of babies," says Ma.

They is all ready to go but the fancy car won't start. McVey look under the hood and wants to know who the hell took off with the distributor, but we all say we don't know much about cars, and maybe the kids been playing with it or something.

We borrow Louis Coyote's pickup again and drive them to catch the bus at Hobbema Crossing. Illianna she real quiet and look at us like we cow chips or something. McVey, he say Wounded Knee gonna look like a picnic when he gets through with us. I think he even say he gonna write his MP.

Next morning a whole string of cars come up the road into the reserve. There is the big white tow truck from Wetaskiwin, a car full of RCMP and about eight guys in suits and hats who look just like Brother Bob. They move right along and we barely have time to tear the culvert out by the slough so they have to walk up to the houses.

Eathen, he be with the fancy car, about eight miles back in the hills. It funny, but all of a sudden, today, none of us speak English very much.

We never heard of anybody named Eathen Firstrider, and the Ermineskins all moved away a long time ago, to Calgary, maybe.

Cars? No, we ain't got no cars. One old pickup truck around sometimes, but it down to the rodeo at Drumheller for a week or so. They all finally go away shaking their heads and saying how dumb we are.

Illianna write to us to say we better send back the car or she never have anything to do with us again. But we know she don't stay mad with us forever.

She write again in a few months to say she gonna have a baby. You think that don't get a celebration. Me and Ma and Eathen borrow the truck, load Mad Etta in the back and go to Wetaskiwin. We set Etta on her two chairs together at the Alice Hotel and buy her lots of beer.

Illianna sends us a little white card when the baby come. A boy, they call him Robert Ermineskin McVey. He looks like Ma, say Illianna.

Everybody counts their fingers and sure enough it's within about a week of when she was home. We have another celebration. Everybody they shake hands with Eathen Firstrider, and give drinks to Mad Etta. Everyone is very much proud that Illianna have an Indian baby.

All us guys learned to drive in the fancy car. It got the muffler torn off and pretty well shot to hell by now, but Eathen still drives everybody around the reserve in it.

I'm not so sure anymore that it is such a funny thing that I have written about, but if it gets me a job with the tractor company, then I guess it is okay.

Dance Me Outside

Little Margaret Wolfchild got murdered down to Wetaskiwin one Saturday night last fall. She wasn't little like most people would think of little. She already eighteen and she got a baby herself about two years ago. She got called Little Margaret because when she born, Moses Wolfchild, what with ten or eleven kids at home, forgot he got a daughter named Margaret. So she is called Little Margaret and the one they got already is Big Margaret. Big Margaret growed up and moved to Calgary five or six years ago and nobody ever heard of her since.

Margaret, she been to the Blue Quills Dance Hall at Hobbema Crossing on Saturday night and sometime after midnight she left with some white guys in a car. They cut her belly with a knife and sort of stuffed her body in a garbage can. Little Margaret she was pretty too. Her face was round and her arms were chubby and she used to wear her hair in braids down her back. She was Robert Coyote's girlfriend when

27

he wasn't off working in the bush.

"I tell you, Silas, we sure as hell gonna have to kill that guy when he get out," Robert says to me.

I don't disagree with Robert Coyote cause he's bigger and older than me and he also waving a very mean looking hunting knife when he say this. Frank and Charlie Fence-post and Eathen Firstrider, they is all there too, and they say we sure as hell gonna kill Clarence Gaskill when he get out of the jail down to Fort Saskatchewan.

After the murder it don't take the RCMP guys long to catch Clarence. Lots of people saw Little Margaret leave in his car. They arrested two other guys with him but let them go cause they said all they did was sit in the car while Clarence and Little Margaret went in the back seat and messed around. Then Little Margaret said something Clarence didn't like and he got mad and killed her. Everybody know Clarence get mean when he drinks. He put the boots to Billy Bigcharles one time and he'd of killed him too if his friends hadn't stopped him. Billy still got a bad arm from that beating.

I don't know much about law even though I go to the Technical School over to Wetaskiwin and I like to read, especially about Indian history. They only charged Clarence with manslaughter. I guess it because Little Margaret was Indian. If she been white it would of been murder for sure. More for sure if it been an Indian guy killed a white girl.

Clarence's Dad, he own the John Deere tractor store in Wetaskiwin, and he hires a lawyer all the way from Calgary. The lawyer's neck folds down over his collar. The jury is all men from Wetaskiwin and there ain't no Indians on it.

They got Clarence's hair cut and dress him up in a suit and tie, and they even bought him a couple of teeth to fill in the hole in his face where he had some teeth knocked out in a fight over to the Alice Hotel beer parlour. When the trial starts, Clarence, he look like one of them religious kids that you see in the park – the ones come from the Lutheran College over to Camrose.

We all went and sat in the back row of the courtroom, wearing our jeans and denim jackets and our hair all blown around cause we had to stand on the highway for a long time every day to hitch a ride into town. Eathen Firstrider, he got a car but he can't take it off the reserve for it don't have no license and neither does Eathen.

That lawyer, he get Clarence to tell his story and he helps him along whenever he gets stuck. It go on for an hour or so and it sound like Clarence a really nice guy and Little Margaret is a bad drunk Indian girl.

The lawyer's words sure sound funny come

out of Clarence's mouth, cause everybody who know him know that Clarence he can't say two words together without cursing. I bet he don't even know what half the words he is saying mean.

They are big lawyer's words that come out of Clarence but what he say is that him and Margaret get to mess around in the car but when their clothes is off Margaret is laugh at him, and to him that a good enough reason to take his knife and kill her.

"Did he say what I think he say?" Robert asks.

"He say he kill Little Margaret cause she made fun of his cock," says Frank. "I gonna bring the shotgun tomorrow."

Frank Fence-post, he been wanting all along to bring a shotgun right into court and blast Clarence good, but Robert Coyote say no, if anybody gonna kill Clarence it gonna be him, but we wait and see what the court do first.

The lawyer, he talk to the jury like they is little kids and he the school principal. He tell them it okay for Clarence to do what he done cause he know that any one of them would get mad too if somebody made fun of their manhood.

Clarence, he blow his nose, wipe his eyes with a big white cloth handkershief, and cry and carry on while he tell his story. He end it by saying he sorry he done it and he wish everyone should forgive him for make a bad mistake.

If what he say was true I be the first one to agree with him, but we all know it ain't. Little Margaret is a girl who laugh lots and be friendly with everyone, even bad dudes like Clarence. We had a murder out to the reserve once, Louis Halter got himself killed, but he deserved what he got. He was all drunk up and he said to Eddy Crow, "I fucked your wife." Yelled it right in Eddy's face. "I fucked your wife and she liked it so much she come back for a couple more times." I mean somebody said that to me about my girlfriend Sadie One-wound, and I had a rifle handy, I'd use it too.

Clarence's friends both tell the same story as him and in the lawyer's words too. A Catholic priest and the Anglican minister both say what a good boy Clarence is. I don't think none of the Gaskell family ever been to a church except for weddings and funerals.

The lawyer gets the court to take a recess after Clarence tell his story, and you can tell by look around that most everybody is sure impressed with how true it is especially that lawyer and the jury.

When we out in the hall Eathen say, "Little Margaret she wouldn't do none of that."

"Yeah, but you think any of them white farmers gonna know that," say Robert.

Frank Fence-post, he took off his jacket the second day of the trial and the court orderly or whatever he is come down the aisle to where we sitting. "Put your jacket on, boy," he says to Frank. "You can't sit in your shirtsleeves in the presence of the Queen."

"I never knew she was here, partner, or I'd of worn my new shirt," says Frank. I figure the guy is gonna throw us all out, but he just look at us like we too ugly to look at and clump back up the aisle.

Since Clarence admit that he done it, the judge tell the jury they got to find him guilty, but when they do they say they recommend mercy.

"Ninety days and a $500 fine," says the judge, and Clarence he smile and shake hands all around before they take him off to jail.

"I'm gonna kill you, you son-of-a-bitch," Robert Coyote says, loud enough for everybody to hear. You can hear everyone draw in their breath real sharp and for a second there is silence until Frank Fence-post says, "Me too."

The RCMP guys herd us all down to the highway and tell us to get the fuck back to the reserve and stay there.

Frank Fence-post he ran the mile from Hobbema Crossing, across the slough and up the hill to where our cabins are. "Clarence Gaskill got out today," he puffed.

Robert Coyote wiped his hunting knife on his jeans.

"We still gonna kill him, right?" he ask.

"Right," says Eathen Firstrider, and everybody else including me, finally. I feel kind of tingly all over and kind of sick at the same time. I never been in a jail, but Robert Coyote has and he say it ain't so bad except you don't get no women. But he say it warm, the food is good and you don't have to work. I think about how we get maybe twenty years and I feel awful scared.

I guess there never was any question that we were going to kill Clarence Gaskell after he got out of jail. We'd sit around our cabin and talk about it and our girls would try to talk us out of it, or tell us at least to try not get caught.

"We all gonna take our guns," says Robert. "Silas, you go down to the dance at Blue Quills tonight. Just keep your eyes open and see who he come with and how they acting. About midnight the rest of us we come down with our guns. You meet us in the bush behind the hall. Then we figure out how we going to get him outside by himself so we can kill him. We don't want to hurt nobody else except Clarence."

"I get to take his scalp," say Frank Fencepost.

"Be careful," says Bertha Bigcharles. Bertha is slim and pretty and would like to be Robert's girl, but he say he don't have no women until he kill Clarence Gaskell.

Sadie One-wound look at me with scared

33

eyes and say, "I don't want you should go to jail, Silas." Sadie is awful special to me. She not very pretty, I guess. She's skinny and got kind of sharp features, but Sadie like to kiss me, and when she hold herself real close to me it sure make me feel strong and brave. I don't say nothing cause maybe I afraid what my voice sound like, but I try to look very solemn.

Some of his friends told Clarence about how Robert Coyote is still saying he going to kill him when he gets home, but Clarence say he not afraid of no fucking Indians, and he be at Blue Quills for the dance, just like old times.

At the dance Clarence is smiling and is strut around like a turkey. He shakes hands on a lot of people and his friends take him back and forth to their cars for drinks quite often.

I watch the big Pepsi-Cola clock above the stage and wait for midnight. Sadie want me to dance with her but I tell her go away. And she does. Clarence is dancing, even with the Indian girls; they laugh with him a lot and I sure don't like to see that.

Along about 11.30 all hell break loose. Somebody come yelling into the hall that Clarence been killed and for somebody to call the RCMP. All the white people and even some of the Indians is gathered around him back behind the parking lot. They say pretty ugly things but they don't know who to be mad at for sure. What I can't figure out is why Robert and Eathen and the other guys don't wait for me like they supposed to. I finally walk down to the bush where they supposed to be and find them just get there.

"What's going on?" they all want to know.

"How come you killed him without waiting for me?" I ask like I real disappointed, but inside I am kind of glad they did.

"We just got here," says Robert. He is carry two rifles and he shove one of them into my hands. About then the RCMP come skidding into the parking lot with their red light turning.

"The Indians are down there in the bush," somebody says, "they're the ones said they were going to kill Clarence." And before we know what happening they got their spotlight on us and we all stand there shielding our eyes while they take away our guns and put hand-cuffs on us.

When we in the back of the police car on the way to Wetaskiwin, the RCMP guys talk about how Clarence was sexually mutilated. They say what a bunch of bastards we were to do something like that to a white man.

Frank Fence-post, he say, "Does sexually mutilated mean he got his balls cut off?" The RCMP guy reach around and just about knock Frank through the back seat.

"I guess it does," Frank whisper into my shoulder, while his nose bleeds all down the front of his shirt.

"Wasn't he shot?" I ask as polite as I know how.

"You should know," says the RCMP.

They questioned all us guys for most of the night, sometimes alone and sometimes all of us together. There was a lot of blood they say, and they got the jacknife that was used on him and they want to know which one of us owns it.

They stamped our fingerprints and took away all of our clothes and even our boots. They say they going to send our clothes to the crime laboratory in Regina, and they say too, that if there is even so much as one drop of Clarence Gaskell's blood on those clothes, or one fingerprint on the knife, they going to charge us all with murder. And they say they don't give a shit how we get back to the reserve with nothing but shorts.

I sure hope Frank ain't got the same blood as Clarence, cause his nose splash on all of us in the back of the car there. Frank ain't worried though, he say Indians got eagle's blood, so they be able to tell the difference easy in a laboratory.

If it hadn't been for the Seventh Day Adventist minister, who give us some blankets and a ride, we'd of all froze. We had to promise to come to his church the next Sunday or he wouldn't of helped us. None of us went, although I thought about it.

None of us guys ever got our clothes back

from the RCMP but I figure that a pretty cheap way not to get charged with murder. When the tests come back from Regina the RCMP is real disappointed that our clothes and boots don't have none of Clarence's blood on them. They questioned all us guys again a few times, especially Robert Coyote, but about all they do is call us bad names and say what they going to do to the guy who done it when they catch him. Nobody ever got charged and they haven't been around for a long time now.

At the dance that night most everybody is dancing all the time but me. I just sit on the bench along the side of the hall and I must of been the only one who seen it was Bertha Bigcharles who danced Clarence outside. I even heard him say it. Bertha was pushing herself up close to him and whispering in his ear, and I hear him laugh and say, "Dance me outside, baby," as they go by me. When I look around the hall I see that my Sadie One-wound and some of the other girls are not there too.

When the minister finally brought us home that night, Sadie is waiting at our cabin. I make her burn her jeans and shoes, and she go and has Bertha Bigcharles, Sandra Coyote, and maybe another couple of girls do the same.

"Hold on to me, Silas," Sadie say to me that night, "and don't let me go for a long time," and her body is tremble and it is a very long time before she finally go to sleep in my arms.

Horse Collars

I was pretty young, nine or ten maybe, the day that Wilbur Yellowknees come home to the reserve. We seen his wagon coming up the road that lead to our place from Hobbema Crossing and the highway. I figured it sure was somebody important because the harness was all decorated with red ribbons and the collars on the horses were the brightest yellow I ever seen.

Papa, he come out of the cabin and I stand behind him in the yard and watch the wagon rumble up the hill. My sister Illianna is peek around the cabin door and she hold onto the hand of Joseph, my brother. He older than me but he had the scarlet fever when he just a baby and his mind, they say, is never gonna grow up like mine and Illianna's.

"By God!" say Papa. "It's Wilbur Yellowknees and his girls," and he walk down the road a bit to meet them.

There are two grey horses pull the wagon, which is got a big box made out of planks on it with canvas over the back part of the box. I sure figure that Wilbur Yellowknees must be even a city Indian because he wearing a suit. It a black cloth suit and he got a round black hat on his head and his hair be in braids down his back and tied up with red ribbon the same as the horses got on their harness.

The kids come out from the other cabins and stand around look shy at the pretty ribbons and yellow horse collars. Our horses got collars too, but they only black leather and they all worn so the horse-hair stuffing is fall out in lots of places.

They talk some about the weather and Wilbur say they been down Red Deer way for a long time now and that they even lived in Calgary for a while. He is wear a cherry-coloured western shirt and I sure wish I have one like it.

Wilbur he got his two daughters with him. They stay in the back of the wagon box and talk and laugh to each other. They are Celina and Gladys he tell us. Celina is old, sixteen or so already, she is chubby and have a round face, and she got braids with red ribbon too. She is wear blue jeans and a yellow sweater that show she is most a woman. Gladys is maybe twelve and she wear a pale blue dress made out of stuff I seen the bride wear at a white people's wedding down to Wetaskiwin one time.

I figure Wilbur he be a city Indian for sure because he bring out a box of beer and he give Papa and Ma each one, and then he offer me one too, only I guess I look funny with surprise because he laugh and laugh and slap his hand on his back pocket. Then he bring out a big bag of hard candy to pass around for all the kids and I figure he sure must be rich. By the way everyone is glad to see him I guess he used to live here on the reserve, but I don't remember him.

Boy, I sure do like Wilbur Yellowknees. All the kids do. But what is best of all is that Wilbur Yellowknees like me back. All that week I follow him around. He give me extra candy and even some money of my own to spend. One of his horses' bridles is broke pretty bad and he say he let me help fix it.

"I sure wish I had a boy like you," he say, and that sure do make me feel good. My own Papa, he don't wish he had none of us. "Maybe I ask your Pa if you could come live with me and the girls. I bet he like to get rid of you." We laugh about that and he mess my hair some.

Saturday, Wilbur and Papa and Wilbur's girls going to go into Wetaskiwin. I ask Wilbur if I can go too and he say sure, but he wonder if I old enough to drink at the Legion, and everybody is have a good laugh.

At the last minute he decide to leave Gladys at our place. "She ain't no good today," I hear him tell Papa.

That morning when I get up Wilbur's harness is all fixed. I sure surprised when I see what he done. His old bridle is gone and the new one is one I seen before. It belong to Blind Louis Coyote.

"You buy that bridle from Blind Louis?" I ask. Wilbur don't answer for a long time.

"I sort of trade him."

"For what?"

"I give him things."

"What things?"

"Just things," he says with a voice that mean I shouldn't ask no more.

It take a long time to drive the wagon into town and it is evening when we get there. Wilbur tie up the horses in the yard behind the Canadian Legion. Papa and Wilbur go in to drink beer. Celina and me stay there. Celina not happy and she don't like to talk to me. She just sit on the cowhide robe in the wagon box, eat hard candies and smoke cigarettes.

After it dark a while a white man come out of the Legion and walk over to the wagon.

"You the girl?" he say to Celina.

"Yeah," she say. "You got the money?"

"Go away, Silas," she say to me. I don't know where to go so I don't move.

"Give him a quarter," she say to the man.

"How come?" he say. "The guy in there didn't say nothing about paying the kid."

"Just give him some change." The guy looks mean at me but he pull out a whole handful of coins and give them all to me.

41

"Go down to a café or something, Silas."

I find a café and have two hamburgers and a Coca-Cola. I sit around there until the café lady say it time I should leave. On the way back I meet Papa and a bunch of people. They is all laugh and yell a lot.

"Kicked us out of the Legion so we is going to a party," he say. "You wait by the wagon."

It real warm and kind of smell sweet in the dark. I don't want to make Celina mad at me so I creep into the tall grass next to the Legion building. I can hear the music play inside and people laugh a lot and glasses clink. Some more men come out to talk to Celina. After a while I go to sleep.

I sleep for quite a while. I get woke up by some yelling. Most of the cars is gone from the lot and all that left is the wagon and Celina and Wilbur.

"You keep some money," yells Wilbur.

"There was only five guys," Celina yell back.

"Six."

"Five." They are standing beside the wagon. They argue for quite a while and say lots of ugly things to each other.

"I don't care what you say, there was only five guys and I give you the money they gave me," say Celina.

Wilbur, he hit her then. It seem kind of funny to me, because he is the one who hits but he is the one who fall down too, because he drunk. He just roll on his back and get up again real slow, but he forgot about his hat which fall on the grass when he did. Celina is hold her face and cry some. Wilbur, after two or three tries, crawl up in the wagon box and go to sleep.

Celina sit down with her back against a wagon wheel and cry. I want to say something nice to her but I afraid she is mad with me too. I go to sleep again. It already light when Papa come back from his party. He stagger around some then climb up in the wagon.

"Untie the horses," he say to me.

"They Wilbur's horses. They don't know the way home."

"You drive them," says Papa, and goes to sleep beside Wilbur.

Some other time I'd be real happy driving a team all by myself, but right now I feel bad about a lot of things, especially about Wilbur who is snore and groan on the floor of the wagon. One of his braids come undone and he got hair sticking all across his face.

Celina, she sit up and hold the reins while I lead the horses out to the highway. I never notice before how skinny the horses are and they walk always with their heads down. The pretty yellow horse collars are hard when you touch them and there are big sores on the necks where those collars rub.

I am used to Papa get drunk, but I guess I

hope Wilbur was not the same. We a long way out of town when I remember we forgot Wilbur's hat.

Celina's eye be all swelled shut and her cheek kind of yellow coloured. I walk along beside the wagon in the ditch. The grass is wet and my jeans are wet right up to my waist. Once in a while a car goes by on the highway, zip, zip, just like a big dragonfly.

Panache

Me and Frank Fence-post and a few other guys been taking a course the government offer on how to be mechanics. The first year of the course was just about over and Mr. Nichols, our English instructor and counselor was helping some of us write job application letters so we maybe work and earn some money in the summer.

I have to write Frank Fence-post's letters because he is only able to write most of his name.

"Hey, Silas," Frank he say to me, "if we get these letters wrote up all spelled right and all, wouldn't it be better if we could keep them from knowing we is Indians?"

"How we gonna do that?" says Tom Pony. "With names like Silas Ermineskin, Donald Bobtail and Rufus Firstrider, it not going to be so hard for them to guess."

Frank, he finally decide to sign his letters J. Frank Fence-post, so it sound important just like the Mayor of Wetaskiwin, who is Mr. J.

45

William Oberholtzer. We all laugh a lot about that, but Mr. Nichols he say that us guys will maybe get to work in a mill somewhere but they put Frank in Public Relations, whatever that is.

The last talk that Mr. Nichols gave us in English class is one that I never forget. It is Mr. Nichols who get me to write down stories and he say if I keep on maybe someday I write some good enough to get printed.

His lecture was all about a French word called panache, which he say is, and I write it down real careful: "the ability to exude the effect of a plume on a helmet."

He shows us pictures of knights with big curled feathers above their armour, and he tell us that anybody can act like he got them feathers. If we stand tall and have the right attitude then we can have panache and look like we warriors wearing a war bonnet and holding a lance, even if we really just got on jeans and a T-shirt. Then we look at pictures of Indian chiefs and Mr. Nichols say that they got more nobility and panache than knights ever had. I make sure I remember what it is he tells us but I don't figure I have a chance to use it for maybe a long time.

Me and Frank and Tom Pony all got hired by a coal mine out near Jasper, Alberta, and a good long way from our reserve here at Hobbema. The mine is at a place called Luscar, what used to be a town but ain't anymore, and the mine ain't underground like you would suppose but is up top and called a strip mine. The mine is called Cardinal Coal Mines and Frank he figures that it must be owned by Indians. We got about twenty families named Cardinal on the reserve and we guess maybe one of them run it.

The nearest town is called Hinton, and the three of us take the bus up there and get us a basement room and board with a white lady who says we should call her Gran. Her husband runs the movie machine at the picture show and he say he let us guys in free to all the movies.

"That's really white of you," Frank says. I kick his ankle and when we alone I tell him not to make fun of these people cause they is really trying to be nice on us. None of us ever been in a white people's house before – they even got three goldfish in a big glass jar.

Gran, she serves us more food that I ever seen before, and she say she gonna have to fatten us up, especially Tom Pony who is little and got hollow cheeks. She say he looks like he never had a good meal in his life.

Boy, this is sure nice people, and things look good for us until the first day we start work.

We have to take a company bus about 25 miles out to the mine and boy do the guys we gonna work with ever look funny at us on the way out.

"Maybe they don't have no Indians in this

part of the country," whispers Frank.

"Maybe they do," say Tom Pony.

I never even dream there are places like this mine. They got there what they call trucks but they is three men tall and the cab sits off to one side like they missed when they put it together. I am almost six feet tall but I don't even come to the top of one wheel. These trucks go up and down narrow little trails and then back up to the very edge of what sure look like hell to me, and dump their load. The rocks go down, what the foreman say is over 500 feet into a pit that he says been burning for maybe twenty years. There is smoke hang around over everything, make it like it cloudy all the time.

We don't have to drive the trucks and I sure glad about that. We just gonna do odd jobs. That is if we ever get to work, cause when the shifts change everybody have a big meeting with the foreman. We don't have to figure too hard to guess that it about us.

All the men wear bright red coveralls and yellow hats and what with the dust and smoke around all over, it sure remind me of a picture I seen once of all the devils in hell.

"We ain't gonna have no so-and-so Indians work here," says a big man with a beer belly and yellow hair.

"I don't like it no better than you, Gunderson," say the foreman. Then he goes into a long story about how the government gives money to the mine, but if the mine takes the money it got to hire some guys like us.

They argue for a long time. Gunderson say there no way the men gonna work if we work.

"Look," say the foreman, "I'm gonna put the tall one up in the tower with a pencil and the other two on odd jobs. You won't even know they're here."

Gunderson went and had a pow-wow with the other men.

"As long as they don't touch none of the equipment. We don't want them to screw nothing up. It's dangerous enough here without guys like that working on our machines." I can tell right then that we ain't gonna get to do no mechanic work even though that's what we been trained to do for the last year.

"I think they is afraid of us," say Frank. "Should I show them my knife? That Gunderson guy's hair sure look good on my belt."

What happens is we don't get to do much of anything. I count the loads each truck dumps but some other guy counts them too. Frank sweep the floor of the garage and when he finish he sweep it again. Tom Pony stand out near where the trucks back up. He is supposed to wave them back and signal them when to stop which would be an important job except that all the drivers they been working here a long time and they put the truck where they want it and don't pay no attention to Tom except for a couple of them I think tried to run him over once or twice.

"They'll get used to you in a few days," said Gran, while she was packing us the biggest lunches I ever seen with sandwiches made with real ham and fresh tomatoes. We only been here a couple of weeks and already Tom Pony look like he is put on weight.

"You just seem a little strange to them," Gran went on. "Once they get to know you everything will be okay." Gran, she remind me of my Ma who is always believe everything gonna be okay too, no matter how bad it get.

"They is plenty strange to us too," says Frank, "Don't nobody ever think of that?"

Gunderson, he have all the men except us sign their names on a paper sheet that he gonna send to the head office of the mine, so they have to get rid of us.

But the paper it never got sent because that afternoon Gunderson have his accident. I was way up in the tower so all I could do was watch. Gunderson is back his truck up to the edge of the pit but he come up real fast try to scare Tom Pony and go a few feet too far and the rock start to crumble away from under the back wheels. He tries to pull forward but all that keeps the truck from going down is the forward pull of the wheels.

"Jump!" yells the foreman, but Gunderson is all tangled up and hangs there like a monkey on a stick I seen once at the Royal American Shows at the Ponoka Stampede. Some say that Gunderson got his overalls caught on the gearshift or that he had his boot jammed under the brake. It depend who you listen to tells the story, but he is sure one long time getting out of that cab.

What happens next I don't believe if I don't see. Tom Pony been waving him back and he is right at the edge looking at where the rock breaking away. Afterward, everybody say how Tom is a hero and all, and what a good Indian he is because he save Gunderson's life even though he trying to get Tom fired. I don't think Tom even knew who was in the cab. But I put myself in his place and figure that if that truck go over, guess who gonna get blamed, the Indian or the driver? I figure Tom was more trying to save our jobs than anything else, but I never tell anybody else that. It funny how people, even big tough ones like Gunderson and his friends, like to believe in heroes.

Tom Pony he get right out on the edge of the pit dig in his foot and push against the wheel of the truck. I only heard about someone show strength like he did then.

On the reserve they tell about one time Moses Louis rolled his Volkswagen on top of himself and Mrs. Louis she picked it up off him cause she was the only one around and if she didn't he'd of died.

"Jump!" the foreman keeps yelling and someone is climb up and pull on Gunderson's one leg that hangs out the door, but no-one goes back to help Tom Pony. He just pushes against the back wheel and from way up where I am I can tell that for a few seconds that truck stops crawling backward. Those few seconds give Gunderson enough time to untangle and finally he is jump clear. Tom Pony ain't so lucky. He got no place to jump clear to and the rig goes over the bank and takes Tom with it.

That night we is all sit around the bar down to the Timberline Hotel in Hinton. Gunderson is our best friend now and so is just about everybody else. They sure buy us a lot of beer and say what good guys we are. Gunderson say that there should be a memorial of some kind for Tom Pony, even if they never gonna be able to get his body up out of that burning pit. He pass the hat around the bar and collect a whole lot of bills, mostly tens and twenties.

"We're going to buy a stone and put it on the side of the hill by the mine entrance for everybody to see," Gunderson say. Everybody is some happy.

"Hey, Partner," Frank say to me, "you figure they figure if they buy us enough beer it gonna bring Tom Pony back to life?"

Me and Frank went with Gunderson the next morning down to the tombstone place. Gunderson talked to a man in a suit and a bright red tie who pointed out the different stones in the yard.

"This here's the best we can get for the money we got," Gunderson says finally, pointing at a shiny black stone with what looked like little flecks of gold in it.

"It's okay with me," I say. It be better if we give the money to Tom Pony's mother, but I don't say that.

"What do you want on it?" say the man in the suit.

"Why couldn't we just take the stone back with us to Hobbema?" say Frank. "We could take it on the bus. I buy it a ticket myself and it can sit beside me just like Tom Pony did on the way down."

I was trying to think of what to put on the stone.

"His name?" said the man.

"Tom Pony."

"Thomas…"

"No. Just Tom."

"Date of birth?"

Frank and me looked at each other. "He was eighteen," I said.

"You want an inscription? You get up to six words free."

I couldn't think of anything for a while, then I remember Mr. Nichols' last lecture to us.

"Panache," I say.

"What's that?" said the tombstone man,

who was making notes with a pencil in a scribbler.

"It's what I want on Tom Pony's tombstone. Panache."

I had to spell it for him about six times before he got it right.

"What is it anyway, some kind of Indian word?"

"Yeah, I think it is," I say.

Butterflies

Every summer for the last few years Pauline and her friend Winnie Bear is come to visit us on the reserve. Pauline is my Aunt Dorothy's girl and Aunt Dorothy and Uncle Alex they been city Indians for a long time. He works in a mill of some kind in Edmonton and they got a big house just like white people and two cars and both of them run.

Before they come that first time Pauline is say in her letter she gonna bring her girlfriend but she don't say that the girlfriend be white. They is only about twelve or so at that time.

"Her Mom don't like me," says Pauline, "but she glad get rid of Winnie for the summer. She too busy to like Winnie much, they don't get along so good. She say Winnie is crazy like Indian she may as well go live with them."

Winnie be the tallest girl I ever seen. She has skinny long arms and long legs like the sand cranes that live down to the slough. She pale, even for a white girl and have long blond hair, and blue eyes that look right at you when she talk. And she talk lots.

I never know her right name for sure but she know all about our names cause Pauline told her. Pauline's name is Walk-away, and she tell Winnie about me, Frank Fence-post, Elias Standing-at-the-door, and Rufus Firstrider.

"You call me Winnie Bear," she say to us, only she say it like one word.

Ma, she laugh some at this white girl wants to be an Indian, and I think at first she a little afraid this girl is make fun of us, but she say anyway that we is to call her anything she wants because she is our guest. "Usually it is Indians try to be white people," Ma say.

She get the name Winnie Bear from some story her Daddy used to read her when she is little. Her Daddy be a big doctor somewhere but she don't live with him no more. She not like any white girl we ever met before. She is play with everybody, laugh a whole lot and be nice to everyone. When us guys go to Wetaskiwin the white girls make screwed-up faces when we walk by. They call us wagon burners and we never get to touch none of them.

She going to be a doctor, one day, Winnie Bear tells us.

"She so smart in school they move her a couple of grades ahead of where she should be," says Pauline. Winnie Bear is the kind of a girl you believe when she say she going to be a doctor, not like old Pauline who all the time tell us she going to be a movie star or maybe an air-plane pilot.

My friend Rufus Firstrider is sure like Winnie Bear and he is sure proud when she likes him back. That first summer she play doctor on him, and bandage him all over with flour sacks and make splints on his arms and legs just like she seen her Daddy do on real people.

"When you get big you going to be my girlfriend, alright?" say Rufus. And that kind of funny because Winnie Bear is already lots taller than Rufus, who is skinny and real dark and has black hair that is always fall all over his face.

Winnie Bear laugh and say sure she be Rufus' girlfriend and that she sure have one long name when it be Winnie Bear Firstrider. But she don't say it mean and we is all sure happy for Rufus.

I just hope that Winnie Bear know what she is saying. Rufus he believe her when she say she going to be his girl. It mean she is promised to him and that probably someday they be get married. It is kind of a custom with us, like I ask Sadie One-wound to be my girl a long time ago, and everybody know that we get married one day.

Rufus is start building his own cabin last fall, then he work most of the winter in the lumber camp and finish it this spring. It is up on the hill about a quarter of a mile behind our place.

It only got two rooms and no furniture but an old cook stove and a mattress on the floor, but Rufus say that it going to be his and Winnie Bear's place. Rufus he be almost twenty now, and I guess Winnie Bear sixteen or seventeen, so he figure when she come visit this summer she not going back to the city.

Winnie Bear she like butterflies. So Rufus he found some stickers like stamps in the Metropolitan Store in Camrose, only they got pictures of butterflies on them instead of the Queen. He stick them all around the windows and on the walls some. He also got a necktie that on the tag say it handpainted and it got butterflies on it too. Some of our friends who don't know Winnie Bear very good call her the Butterfly Girl. Boy, Rufus can't wait to show her that tie. I really like Winnie Bear, but I sure hope she not going to disappoint Rufus or nothing.

Pauline and Winnie Bear don't come see us in June like usual. I help Rufus write a letter to Pauline but we don't get any answer.

Those summers when Winnie Bear here, she is sure make it a happy place and everybody is laugh a lot. Winnie Bear is want to catch butterflies and she want we should catch some too, but we never thought to catch none. Butterflies to us is just to look at. Winnie Bear don't have no net – you got to have a net to catch butterflies – she tells us, so she take an old broom handle and a coat hanger that she bend into a circle and then she got a pair of Ma's old underpants and stretch them over the coat hanger and she got her net. Ma, she is laugh and slap her big leg some when she see that skinny white girl running crazy with them big long legs of hers. She don't give up even when she fall down a lot. She just get up, look at her scratches and run some more.

She puts the butterflies she catches in an old anti-freeze tin and peek at them every little while until they don't flutter no more. Then she take a pin and sticks it through them and pins them to the back of the old stuffed chair in our house. By the end of the summer she have the back of the chair most covered. I don't like much to see her pin them though. I watched a doctor cut some glass out of my finger once and when I look at his face I can see that he enjoying himself doing that. Winnie Bear is the same. The butterflies make a crunch sound when she sticks the pin through their head. I don't see how someone can stick pins in something as pretty as that, that don't do nobody no harm. But, if it make Winnie Bear glad then I guess I glad too.

Last summer when they here, they is both grown up some. Winnie Bear don't catch butterflies only once. Her and Pauline is more interested make party than stay around the reserve so much. They go down to the highway and hitch-hike rides into Wetaskiwin or maybe down to Ponoka. There, they run around with white guys who got big cars. The white guys buy them lots to drink and sometimes they don't get back until near morning. It not a very happy time for Rufus Firstrider.

One night, Rufus and me and Frank Fencepost is pull up the culvert on the road up to our place and when they come home those white guys is drive right into it. They all stand around look dumb at their car. We walk down and offer for $20 to borrow Louis Coyote's pickup and pull them out. They is some mad but they know that if they leave the car they likely never see it again and anyway the tow truck won't come out to the reserve for nobody. Winnie Bear think what we done is real funny and she hug Rufus' neck right there in front of that carload of white guys and tells them, "Give my friends here $20." That sure make Rufus proud.

Pauline she figures she going to marry one of them white guys but all of a sudden he don't show up no more and I hear her talk to Winnie Bear that she real worried whether they make a baby or not.

By the middle of July Rufus he real worried cause it look like Winnie Bear never going to come back. We go down to the pay phone at the store at Hobbema and we phone my Aunt Dorothy in Edmonton. She say she don't know where Pauline is, that her and Winnie Bear got a place of their own last fall and she never come around no more, and just as well cause they a couple of bad ones.

Rufus and me figure maybe in a week or so we go to Edmonton and look for them. But a couple of days later one of the kids comes running up from the highway and say that Pauline and her friend get off the bus and that we better come help them cause something be wrong.

Me and Rufus Firstrider we borrow Louis Coyote's pickup and drive down to the crossing. We is some surprised at the way they are: Pauline is look like she really old with her face all pinched and hurting, while Winnie Bear is sit on the porch of the store, look at her feet and don't notice us.

Pauline is start to cry when she see us, and Rufus is talk to Winnie Bear but she don't even let on he is around.

"She's awful sick," says Pauline. "We take her to your place. Okay, Silas?"

Winnie Bear look like she ain't ate for a long time and her eyes look like they been painted on her face and not a part of her no more. Pauline pulls real hard on Winnie Bear's arm and she get up and follows Pauline a few steps then she stop until Pauline is pull on her arm some more.

We get back to our place and sit Winnie Bear in the old stuffed chair. She just look at our busted TV like it got a show on it, and she is never spoke one word.

Rufus, he sits on his haunches in front of her and tries to get her to notice him. It sure is sad to see his face.

"Mad Etta will make her better when she gets back to the reserve," Rufus is say quite a few times.

"I been thinking about that too," says Pauline. "Mad Etta she done some wonderful things with sick people."

Mad Etta she weigh 300-400 pounds, take five flour sacks to make her a dress. She know more about medicine than all them white doctors been to a university. She goes out on the full moon, dig roots, pick leaves and stuff. Then she boil different kinds together to make medicine. She cures the stiff backs and sick stomachs, and when the white doctors say David Calf-robe gonna die with the polio she is bury all but his face in the ground she soaked with her medicine. David is most old as me now and walk with only one little limp. Another time Mad Etta make medicine get my sister Illianna have a baby even though she take the birth control pill.

"White man's medicine weak," Etta says all the time.

We tease her she should do medicine dance like old time medicine man. "Etta too big to dance," she say, and she laugh and laugh, shaking all over on the tree-trunk chair in her cabin.

We sure wish Etta is here now to fix up Winnie Bear, but she away to a rodeo down Claresholm way, where she cook for Charlie Fence-post's chuckwagon outfit. She be back in a week or so, maybe.

Everybody is just sit around and don't know what to say. Ma, she makes Winnie Bear some tea but she don't drink it even when we hold it right under her nose. We want to ask Pauline lots of things, but we know she tell us when she ready. Rufus has gone got his butterfly tie and he wave it for Winnie Bear to see but she don't.

"Will you make some porridge, Silas?" Pauline is say to me. "I got to feed her or she'll die. She don't do nothing but sit like that all the time. She been like that for two months now. The Welfare, they say they going to put her in the place for crazy people. I can't let them do that so I take her down to the bus station and we come here. I don't know nothing else to do."

And then Pauline she start to cry lots, and Ma take her in her arms and she sits on Ma's big knee and sob like she was a little girl again.

It is a really hard job to feed Winnie Bear the porridge. The first time Rufus hold her nose and I try to poke the spoon in her mouth. But she is only open her lips not her teeth and the porridge goes all over her pretty yellow sweater.

"You got to pry her mouth open," Pauline says.

So Rufus pry her teeth apart and I slip in the

spoon. Once she get food in there she is chew it up okay. Pauline is smile just a little bit cause she can see me and Rufus can feed her good.

Pauline tell us that her and Winnie Bear left their homes last fall after they went back to Edmonton. Winnie Bear quit school even though she is about the smartest one there, but she can't get along with her mother no more and her daddy who live in the East somewhere don't want her. They get a room of their own downtown and make party more than anything else and don't ever keep a job for very long.

"Sometimes it was fun and sometimes it was awful scary," Pauline says. She say they do some pretty bad things all through them months in the winter, but the worst is when Winnie Bear is take something bad that Pauline say, "blow her mind."

Winnie Bear's Mom don't want her around no more and she blame Pauline for Winnie Bear get sick and she chase Pauline right out of their house. And even Aunt Dorothy and Uncle Alex don't want Pauline back if Winnie Bear with her cause they blame her for get Pauline in trouble. Pauline is have her baby in May, she says, and give it out to be adopted.

I guess my aunt and uncle are city Indians for sure. I expect white people turn out their family like that but not Indians. With us here, it don't matter what you done, it always okay for you to come back home.

Ma, she rock Pauline like a baby and pretty soon she go to sleep and when she do she is look young again.

I look at Pauline sleep and I think on Winnie Bear sit so quiet and pretty. She sure like one of them butterflies been caught. Somebody stick a needle in her and she just sit still like the butterflies she used to pin to the back of our old stuffed chair.

Rufus, he look at Winnie Bear with love all over his face. He take his red handkerchief out of the back pocket of his jeans and wipe the porridge off Winnie Bear's sweater. He touch her so soft like maybe she break easy.

The McGuffin

On the way to Calgary with my friend Frank Fence-post to visit my sister Illianna, I bought a movie magazine at the bus depot in Red Deer. My English instructor and counselor at the Tech School, Mr. Nichols, say I should read a whole lot and that make me able to write better than I do.

The magazine tell all about how Elizabeth Taylor and Richard Burton going to get divorced again, but I sure don't see how that going to help me write stories.

There is one thing I remember from that magazine though. I tore it out and put it in the pocket of my jean jacket. It about Alfred Hitchcock the movie man and how he have something in every picture he make called a McGuffin. Mr. Hitchcock say a McGuffin is the thing everybody get all hot and bothered about, like a diamond that been stolen or some secret papers that been lost.

I not sure if a person can be a McGuffin or not, but while we in Calgary we lose Illianna's baby for a while, and boy everybody sure get hot and bothered about that, especially Illianna's white-man husband, Robert McGregor McVey.

He the only one home when we get to their apartment building, which has a lock on the door and a talk-back machine to call the apartments. I got Illianna's address wrote down real careful on the back of a cigarette package and I tell the cab driver be sure and not take us the long way there.

My brother-in-law let us in but we can tell he sure not so happy to see us. Guess he holds a grudge cause a couple of years ago he come home with Illianna once and he kind of lose his car while he there at the reserve. Also he don't know, but we sure somebody else make Illianna's baby with her.

"Would you guys like a drink or something?" Brother Bob say to us. "Illianna will be home soon. She took Bobby over to her girlfriend's."

"Yeah! Me likum firewater," says Frank. There is something about just being around Brother Bob that bring out the bad in Frank and me. I think it is that my brother-in-law don't know how to make laugh. He never know when we is tease him. He expect us to act like movie Indians and we try to act like he expect us to.

Brother Bob get ice and glasses from behind

their bar which is all covered in white leather.

"Don't bother with no glasses. We is just drink out of the bottle," says Frank, and he take the bottle right out of McVey's hand and take a big drink. Then he spit whisky half way across the room, choke for a long time, and tears run down his face. I don't think Frank have whisky more than a couple of times before.

"I have mine in a glass, Brother Bob," I say.

"I think maybe I have a beer," choke Frank.

"Well, how are things out at the happy hunting ground?" say my brother-in-law.

"Oh, you know," say Frank, "pretty quiet. Last week Silas, he killed a couple of RCMP guys come around looking for moonshine. We burned up a wagon train and took twenty white man's scalp."

Brother Bob he look at Frank like maybe he believe him, and run quick get him an ashtray. McVey he don't smoke and I guess Illianna don't anymore either, cause there is no ashtray anywhere and Frank he rubbing his ashes into the knee of his jeans.

When Illianna come in the door, Brother Bob say, "Hey, Illianna, look who's here! Your brother Si and Frank Post-hole."

"Fence-post," say Frank.

"Whatever," says Brother Bob.

Illianna she glad to see us. The baby is sure cute, and just like we suspect, he sure look like Eathen Firstrider, Illianna's old boyfriend, and not like her white man at all.

They sure got one fancy apartment. It a lot nicer even that the Alberta Hotel in Edmonton where I stay the night once. There is carpet everywhere and the furniture look like it just come from a store window.

The baby, his whole name is Robert Ermineskin McVey, is not make shy at all. Mostly he like Frank though. Frank is make funny face, roll his eyes like he drunk and click his tongue sound like a woodpecker. Little Bobby is smile from one ear to the other and reach out to Frank.

Brother Bob he sort of start to stop Illianna from handing the baby, but he don't when he see she smiling. The baby is hug and kiss Frank a lot, pull his long hair and say "Da Da" to him. I think Brother Bob like to pour hot water over both of us before we touch that baby.

Me and Frank and Illianna stay up real late talk about old times on the reserve at Hobbema before Illianna come to the city and marry her white man. Illianna even have a cigarette with us. She say Bob don't like her smoke around the baby no more cause it bad for him.

"I don't have no bed for you guys," Illianna say.

"Hey, we sleep right here on the carpet," says Frank. "Boy, it softer than my bed any day."

Brother Bob already gone to work when we

wake up the next day. Illianna she make up a big breakfast for us. She say that they going to buy a big house pretty soon so that Bobby have a yard to play in.

"You should move back to the reserve. We got more yard there than anything else," says Frank.

We figure to go downtown to look in the pawn shops for a while so we ask Illianna if it okay we take little Bobby with us. She say it okay as long as we back by five o'clock when her husband come home from work.

It been snow some and the streets is all slippery. Illianna get the baby wrapped up in a yellow snow suit so he look like one of them toys in the store windows.

We hardly get off the bus downtown when Frank's boots with the metal heels slip on the slushy sidewalk. Lucky he fell backward cause he slide about 50 feet on his back in the wet with Bobby held tight to his chest. He is some mess when he stop. A white man help him up. "You drunk, or what?" the guy says to him.

"I just taking this here kid for a ride, mister."

The baby is clap his yellow mittens together and kiss Frank.

"Sure be nice if we would have a beer," says Frank, and I agree. We down by the Queen's Hotel where all the Indians hang around. We been looking around in pawn shops cause

Frank he like to buy an electric guitar or maybe a tape recorder.

"We ain't got electricity at home," I say.

"It okay, Silas, I like them cause they look pretty."

We go in the Queen's beer parlour, but we just sit down when the waiter come over say we can't bring in the baby.

"Don't worry," says Frank. "We don't let him drink more than two beers or he get mean and bust up the place." That waiter he don't figure it funny and tell us to get our tails out of there.

Back on the street we is walk by the A-1 Speedy Taxi Co. Ltd. They have a little waiting room face right on the street and a real pretty girl is sitting in there. She look out, smile, and motion for us to come into the waiting room. She sure is one pretty girl and she is smile nice at me. I figure it because I wearing my new cherry coloured western shirt with five pearl buttons up each sleeve and a button about every half inch down the front.

"You want to go out?" she say to me.

"Well, sure," I say. "I just get to town though and I don't know my way around too good. Where would you like to go?" She sure look at me kind of funny.

"I mean are you looking for a girl. It's $20 for me and $3 for the room. Right across the street there at Buffalo Rooms."

71

"We just looking for somebody to watch the baby for us," I tell her. Boy, she is wearing a short red skirt and white boots up to her knee. I sure wish I have $23 I don't need. I sure wish I have $23 at all.

Becky, she tell us her name is, look at the baby. He smile on her and she holds him a minute.

"Cute little bugger, ain't he?" says Becky.

"We let you hold him for nothing," says Frank. "We just go for a quick beer over to the Queen's Hotel."

"Well. . ." she says, "Okay, but make it quick. This is Friday and business is usually good Friday afternoons. If I get a trick I'll leave him with the dispatcher there," and she points behind a glass wall at a grey-haired lady who is talk to the taxi men on a radio. She holds up the baby and he and the lady grin at each other. "Jesus, but Indian babies are cute," says Becky.

Over at the Queen's beer parlour we right away meet Herbert Thomaset, Suzie Calf-robe and some other people used to live on the reserve. They is all happy to see us and they buy us beer and we talk about old times. We don't drink a lot but we sure talk some and boy the time goes by fast. We don't neither of us have a watch but when Herbert Thomaset say, "I got to be going home, it's seven o'clock," we sure decide we better go get our baby.

It already dark out and boy Illianna gonna

be mad on us and I not even want to think about Brother Bob. Us Indians always have trouble with time. It just that if we say we going to go someplace we don't mean right now like a white man do when he say that. We mean maybe in two-three days or a week. But I bet that Illianna thinks in white time now.

On the way to the taxi office we stop at the pawn shop so Frank can look at the guitar again.

"You guys in some kind of trouble?" the pawn shop man say to us. "There was a little guy in here looking for the baby you had, and he was some upset."

"Did he have a suit, a little hat with no brim, and toe rubbers?" I say. The guy nods to all these.

"I think we know who it is," say Frank.

"He looked like a cop," say the pawn shop man, "so I didn't tell him the time of day. You sure you guys didn't steal that baby somewhere?"

Becky ain't nowhere around the taxi office. "Probably Brother Bob found the baby already," says Frank. "Why don't we just go back over to the Queen's Hotel and hope your brother-in-law don't come look for us with a gun."

The lady dispatcher ain't there either. There is a fat black man smoking a cigar.

"Where is the lady with grey hair?" I ask,

tapping on the glass to get him to look at me.

"Vi? She was off at five o'clock."

"We left a baby in a yellow snow suit here a while ago. . ."

"Yeah. Vi had him but she didn't know what to do with him so she phoned Becky over at the Love Shop and she come and got him. There was another guy looking for the kid too. He looked like a plain clothes dick so I told him to try the police station up on Eighth Avenue."

"Brother Bob sure get around don't he?" says Frank.

"Is the Love Shop something like Buffalo Rooms?" I ask.

"No," says the black man. "It's a place up on Third Avenue sells vibrators and kinky stuff. But the real business is in the back room. There's a bunch of high rollers in town and they're playing poker over there. Becky's there in case they want to take a break from the cards and I guess the baby's there too, if that plain clothes cop ain't found it yet. Hop in the cab out front, it's only about a buck ride."

We get out of the taxi in front of the Love Shop. The window is full of mechanical peckers.

"Don't white guys have none of their own?" says Frank.

I just shake my head.

"Hey, Silas, there's Eathen Firstrider," says Frank pointing to one about a foot long. "And

74

there's Robert Coyote," he say, pointing at another big one.

"And there's Frank Fence-post," I say, pointing at a real baby one is hang from a bracelet.

"No. That belong to Illianna's white husband," and we sure do have a good laugh about that.

"Can I help you gentlemen?" says the man behind the counter. He is skinny with a face like a weasel.

"Well we lost our baby and somebody told us he play cards in your back room," says Frank.

"He real short and wearing a yellow suit," I say.

For once a white man knows when we make a joke.

"Yeah, I seen him," he say, "He come in with a hooker named Becky. She said he's the best trick she's turned this month."

The guy, whose name is Sam take us to the back room where there is a round green table with a light over it and eight-nine guys play cards. There is some other guys watching and one of them is hold Bobby.

"See, he not lost after all," says Frank.

Becky come out from behind a curtain at the back of the room, pulling up her boots and pulling down her skirt.

"Shit, it's about time you guys showed up,"

75

she say.

"We want to thank you for look after our baby," I say. "How much do we owe you?"

"Well the babysitting was free, but the horny little bugger sawed off two pieces so you owe me $40." Everybody have a good laugh about that.

Me and Frank is sit on the corner watch the guys play cards. They bet more money on each hand than I ever seen before. When Becky not busy in the bedroom she is get us all a drink and her and Frank is play with the baby. Little Bobby is laugh lots and Becky is get him a handful of poker chips to play with. He throws them around and tries eat them.

There is a tough-looking man with a bald head and chest like a tree trunk. "Bring the kid over here," he growl. "Maybe the little bugger'll bring me good luck. He can't make it any worse." Bobby he don't mind as long as there plenty chips to play with.

"Get the kid a sandwich," says the bald man to Becky, and she just doing that when Brother Bob bust through the door with Sam, the guy who runs the Love Shop, hanging on his arm.

"Where's my baby?" he yell. Then he see me and start for me, but I just point at the table where Bobby is sit on the bald man's knee eat on half a ham sandwich and some poker chips.

Just then two big cops and a guy who look like a wino but is really a detective come crash

76

into the room. "Leave the money where it is and line up against the wall. Everybody's under arrest."

I just guess that what Brother Bob has done is when he find out where Bobby is he call the police to come help him rescue his baby, but when the policeman hear the address they know it is the gambling place so they quick make up a party to raid it.

"We just watch the game," say Frank. "We don't even know how to play cards."

"You kids can't even afford to be in the same room with these guys," says one cop.

"And I'm just here to get my baby," says Brother Bob.

The bald man is stand with one arm lean on the wall, the other arm hold Bobby.

"I bet this one is Montana Shorty," says the detective, pointing at Brother Bob. "I heard he was supposed to be coming up here for a big game."

"That's my baby," say Brother Bob starting over for Bobby who is busy smear butter all over his face.

"Hands on the wall," says one cop. "I suppose you can prove that's your baby," he say in a tired voice.

"Of course I can."

I go over and take the baby from the bald man and go back to the corner.

"It don't look like no big deal to me," say

the big cop. "That there's an Indian baby, and them are Indians." He points at me and Frank. "So give them their baby."

"It's my baby," wails Brother Bob in a real high voice.

"Sure it is," says the big cop, "and are you the mommy or the daddy?"

"He's my son," Brother Bob insist, "and the tall one over there is my brother-in-law Si, and the other one is his friend, Frank Post-hole."

"Fence-post," say Frank.

"Whatever," say Brother Bob. "They can't be trusted," he goes on. "They bring my baby into a room full of criminals... "

"They ain't been arrested for nothing," says the cop.

"I'm the one who called you," squeals my brother-in-law.

"Sure you are, Montana. Some guys will do anything to keep from getting busted." Then he say to us, "You guys get on out of here with your baby, and don't be keeping such bad company after this."

"What about her?" I say, looking at Becky. "She was kind of look after the baby for us."

"Yeah, well we know what you do for a living, honey, but we can't save the whole world in one evening. We're just busting the high rollers tonight, so run along."

"I want my baby," yells Robert McGregor McVey. The cop looks mad.

"Take the baby over to him," he say.

I do, and Bobby is all smiles. He like everybody. But Frank is start click his tongue the way Bobby likes and he turn his head to look at Frank. The more I try to hand him to Brother Bob the more he look at Frank and then he start to cry. Frank come over, take him and the baby put his arms around Frank's neck and give him a butter-faced kiss.

"Get out of here, you guys," the cop says, and to McVey, "You should be ashamed trying to pull a trick like that. Is this guy the baby's father?" says the cop to us.

"No he ain't," says Frank. And I nod. I know we telling the truth but I still feel a little bad about it.

As we leave McVey is yell a lot about who he knows on the police force and what gonna happen to them cops if they don't let him go.

"Shut up, Montana!" say the big cop picking the money up off the table.

We take a taxi back to Illianna's and give her the baby. She is some glad to see him but she say she know we look after him good.

"Did you see Bob?" she say. "He went looking for you."

"Well, yeah, we did," say Frank.

"He run into some people," I say. "I think he be real late get home tonight, and I think what we should do is get home tonight too. So we gonna catch the next bus for Hobbema."

That's what we do too, but on the way I stop off at the Buffalo Rooms for a while to collect the reward I been promised by Becky.

Caraway

*... in some of the Northern tribes the cara-
way plant was believed to hold supernatural
powers ... the placing of the white bloom of
the plant on the eyes of a dying or recently
deceased person was believed to condemn
the spirit to eternal fire....*

— Tales of the Great Spirit

I was about twelve the fall that Ruth Buffalo
killed herself. One shot from the .22 gun her
father, Joe Buffalo, keep in the back bedroom
of their house was all it took.

Ruth, I guess, was most smart Indian girl
ever come from around our place. She was the
only Indian kid around who didn't live on the
reservation. They say there was a big stink by
the white people when she went to their school
instead of to the Indian Affairs school on the
reserve. She got better marks than white kids
and the government end up paying her way
clear through university because she so smart.
She is study to be a teacher, and the kids who

had her — she come back and teach us Indians at the reserve school even though she could have gone about anywhere she wanted — say she is best teacher they ever had. She even speak our language and the kids in her class don't hate school much as everybody else does.

But she killed herself anyway. What I hear from Joe Buffalo a lot later is she stay late to school one night and something is happen to her on the way home. She is run into her house and scream and cry to her Papa that she been had by a farmer live across the field aways, Mr. Russell Bevans. Old Joe try talk to her but she is gone crazy in her mind. "I be dirty forever, Papa," she say to him, "forever and ever." And then she run to the bedroom and shoot herself.

Old Joe Buffalo he no ordinary Indian. He not a reserve Indian. He is own his farm across the highway from the reservation. Old Joe, he old enough to be around when reservation is made up and even way back then he have so much pride he say he not take nothing he don't earn with his own hands. He bought the land so long ago nobody remembers how he got the money.

"I a funny old bugger," he used to say to me. "That's what people in town say. They figure cause I old I don't hear. And they figure at the bank that cause I can't write my name I can't count. Them girls try lots of times give me less than I should have." Joe too old to farm no more but he rent his land and get paid for it.

Nobody like Old Joe much. Reserve Indians don't like that he don't be like them: do nothing; and the white people sure not like it that he thinks he can be same as them. That's what the white people think ... Old Joe, last thing he ever wants to do is be white.

Everybody wonder about him some and like most kids I wonder too. When I about ten me and my friend Frank Fence-post go sneaking around his place. We crawl down from the highway on our bellies and make pretend we are tracking buffalo and that make it a big joke to us.

We crawl right up to back of house and boy we is some proud of ourself, when all of a sudden I feel something cold on the back of my neck, and there be Old Joe Buffalo with his shotgun. I don't know how he got there ... I never hear nothing.

Frank he see what happen to me and he break and run. Old Joe turn and fire the shotgun at Frank, but I see he shoot way up in the trees make sure he don't hit him. Frank he yell like he been hit anyway and run until we hear him hit Old Joe's barbed-wire fence really hard.

"What you do sneak around like a thief?" he say.

"We don't mean nothing. We play at track buffalo."

Old Joe smile a little on me. "You just been

caught by oldest Buffalo in this part of country," he say, and I look at him and see his face is all brown and wrinkled up like Eathen Firstrider's hand-tooled chaps. "Who are you?" he ask.

"Silas Ermineskin," I say. For some reason I don't know, I not scared of him at all.

"You never do nothing but scare away game wearing white man's shoes," and he look at my running shoes whith my toes hang out. "Soft as moss," he say, and point at his own moccasins. "If you drink tea, Silas Ermineskin, you can come in my cabin."

He got on an old red and black mackinaw that he wear everyday for years. His face all wrinkled up but his eyes clear and shiny like a little kid's. His pipe poke out of his mackinaw pocket, and that what his house smell like, his pipe. He don't smoke tobacco but bunch of leaves and roots he collect himself. All the furniture in the house Old Joe make himself is what he tells me.

"You like to learn track game like real Indian?" he ask me.

"Sure I would," I say. "And do ceremony dances and make mean face with war paint. Could you learn me that too?"

"If you want I teach you." He pour us out tea that he cook in a tin pan on the woodstove. He tell me some stories then about when he was a boy and there hardly any white men in our country and it not even called Alberta then. And he tell me about his daughter and how proud he is of her going to graduate the university that year. Old Joe tell me he was 70 when Ruth born and already work on his third wife who was only twenty or so. When Ruth is about two her and her Momma take the measles and the Momma is die. I count in my head and figure that he most 95 years old.

"I hear your family coming to look for you," he says then. I forgot all about Frank and how I been there all day already.

"I don't hear nothing," I say.

"Be quiet! Be still as post and stretch your ears out."

I don't hear nothing even when I stretch my ears, but in a few minutes my Pa, Sam Standing-at-the-door, Frank and some other kids is come through the trees. Pa is carrying his rifle.

They is happy to see me okay, but my Pa tell me, "Silas, don't you never go back there. He's crazy old man thinks he too good for us Indians." So of course I go back every time I got a chance.

Old Joe he don't read or write but he is look around him and understand lots. He say us Indians got to go forward or backward. Our people is gonna die, he say, if we sit still like we do now on the reserves.

"Look at our women," he used to say.

"They don't like be called squaw no more. They drink beer, ride around in white man's cars. Our women the most proud and feared anywhere around at one time. It hurt my heart to see them now. And the men sit around all day curse the white man with one hand take his money with the other."

I think of Chief Tom Crow-eye who is most of the time wear a suit and go to meetings in Edmonton and Calgary. Yet nothing ever change for us.

Old Joe and me get to be great friends. I spend a lot of time there and he tell me the stories his Mama used to tell him about how the Great Spirit make the land and the people and all that.

"I get signed up by the missionaries long time ago," he say like he don't feel quite right about it. "I do it for my old squaw. She is want to believe in white man's God so I say okay. The church people say we got to believe only their way and forget ours. So I never be what they call a religious man. Ruth, she good Catholic. Go to church three times on Sunday. I'd rather lay out muskrat traps."

We is all, most of us Indians, Catholic. A long time ago the missionaries come around get everybody join up the church though most people don't understand what it is all about.

Somebody asks us what religion we are, we say, "Catholic ... I guess."

Even when Ruth come home to teach I hardly ever see her. She is always stay late to the school or work sometimes for the church.

Then come the time Ruth is kill herself. Poor Old Joe, it sure hurts him to be Indian then. He walk to the store at Hobbema Crossing and call the RCMP but they take four-five hours before they come. Old Joe tell them what happened but they don't hardly listen to him, he says.

"I tell them it Russell Bevans done it, but they just make faces to each other like I don't know anything," he tells me.

Russell Bevans he look like a giant to me, then. I guess he was six foot or so with big wide shoulders and a head like a basketball with thin red hair on top. His eyes was pale blue and close together like a pig. His hands make five or six of mine, big like baseball gloves with big black fingernails. He chew snuff, "snoose" he call it, and it was what you smell about him when he come close to you. Everybody know he been after Indian girls lots of times before. Some he get, some he don't. Some older girls go with him for maybe five dollars after they been to town drinking.

The RCMP guys talk to Russell Bevans. He say he don't know nothing about Ruth, and his wife, a scared little white lady with grey hair, say he been home in the yard all that day, and his son say so too, he is about fourte, fat, like to beat up Indian kids, and got the same pig face as his Pa.

Nobody ever thought to have a doctor look at Ruth. She just an Indian.

In town I hear ladies talk in the Co-op Store.

"That Ruth was kind of an uppity one," they say, "and kind of strange like her father. She was probably up to no good of some kind. Had something to hide."

"I bet," said another one, "that if they checked her out they'd find she was pregnant. Indian girls are like that. And imagine her accusing Russell, why he'd give you the shirt off his back, and he hasn't missed church in ten years."

The worst for Old Joe is when the priests from the church say that Ruth can't be buried in the church graveyard because she kill herself. Old Joe swear that everything he say is true. He swear it to the RCMP, the priests, and to me. But I the only one who believe him.

"It not matter to me," he say, "but she care plenty about it. Her spirit not rest unless she be buried there." But it don't matter what he say the church don't change its mind.

Joe is build a coffin for Ruth himself. I never feel more sorry for anyone than him that day. He is just an old man who don't hardly speak the white man language and don't understand why nobody do nothing for his daughter.

He hire two Indians, Rufus Fire-in-the-draw, and Charlie Blanket, to tear down a granary that he don't use no more and pile the boards up against his corral fence. Then he have them put the coffin on top of the boards and he is set fire to all of it. He had went to the church and ask the priests come down and two of them do.

The sun is going down and a storm is blow big clouds across the sky. The fire roars like wind as it burn up against the dark. Old Joe Buffalo is kneel down in the corral, raise his arms to the sky and cry the death song of our people like it been taught to him most a hundred years ago. Charlie and Rufus don't know what to do as they stand by the back of the corral and they finally just sneak away. The priests twist the beads around their necks and the fire flash on their silver crosses and long black robes. After a while they go away making lots of sign of the cross. The fire burn down and all I can hear is the voice of Old Joe Buffalo crying out his sorrow in the fall night.

"I glad you stay, Silas," he say to me when he finally stop. "I going to do something tonight and I don't like to be alone at it."

He bring from the house a Roger's Golden Syrup can and we go back to the fire. There just a few ashes glow a bit like eyes in the dark. Old Joe fill the can up with ashes – if the coals hurt his hands he don't never show it – and then we walk the long miles up the highway to the

Catholic church cemetery and Old Joe is bury that can of ashes there in the graveyard. Then we go back and he makes tea for us. He don't ask me to but I sleep at his house that night.

All that winter I spend a lot of time at Old Joe's. He learns me how to make warpaint and how to set snares and he tell me the legends of our people that almost been forgot by everybody.

"Violets is soft like women's faces," he say, "put violets on a grave and you make the spirit happy."

And he tell me about caraway. I even find that one in a book one time and I print it out at the start of my story so everybody is know Old Joe is tell me the truth.

In the spring he spend a lot of time track Russell Bevans. He get to know where he go every day and what he do. When Bevans is work in his fields Old Joe and sometimes me too, is never far away, but Russell Bevans he never know that. I wonder what it is Old Joe going to do.

In the middle of the summer I come down to Old Joe's place early one morning. Sneak up real quiet like he's taught me to do – Joe is even make for me my own moccasins – and peek through the window. There is Old Joe at the table, naked from the waist up, look in his little square mirror propped on the table and put war paint on his skinny old chest. Then on his face with red, yellow and blue colour is make himself fierce and scary.

Then he put on his mackinaw and go off across the fields to where his land join up with Russell Bevan's land. Russell have private road run along there and he been hauling hay along there with a hayrack and his tractor the last couple of days. I follow way behind so he don't know that I there.

Old Joe gets down in the ditch in the water and wait for the tractor to come along. When it get to maybe fifty feet from where he is, Old Joe take off his mackinaw and rise up out of the ditch like a spirit himself.

Russell Bevans have to either hit Old Joe or turn the wheel. What Old Joe count on I guess is that Russell just be scared and turn the tractor cause I bet he sure like to run over an Indian. He turns the wheel and the tractor tip right over. He make a half try to jump clear but he is too big for that. The tractor is on top of him in the slough water before he know it. He yell some and try to get loose but he is pinned by his chest, hurt a lot and can hardly keep his head above the green water.

"Go get help, you crazy old bastard," he yells at Joe. But Joe is stand look down at him and maybe smile a little. I crawl silent until I right across the road. I lay in the water with the bulrushes and peek across.

"You tell me the truth about my girl," Old

Joe says after a while.

"I don't know nothing," says Russell Bevans, the green water right up to his mouth. "Help me!"

"First you tell the truth. I don't go for help until."

Russell Bevans, he swear and yell. Then he beg Old Joe some to help him. Russell have lots of pain and after a while he make a funny noise and pass out. His head goes under water, but Old Joe wade right in and lift up his head so he don't drown. Then from the pocket of his jeans he take out some caraway flowers and place one on each of Russell Bevans' eyes. He cradle his head like a baby until he wake up. Two or three times this happen until Russell Bevans is finally tell Old Joe, yes, I hurt your daughter. I sorry I done it. If you get me help I'll even tell the RCMP that I done it.

Old Joe Buffalo is smile just a touch and the next time Russell Bevans is pass out Joe don't grab his head. He scatters the last of the caraway flowers on the water above his face and I hear the bubbles come up through the water around them.

Joe goes get his mackinaw and walk real slow away.

"You can walk with me, Silas," he say to me.

"How you know I there?" I say. "I walk real quiet."

"You walk like two moose chased by wolf. I hear you ever since you crossed the highway."

Linda Star

I'd only been in Edmonton maybe three days but I seen her every day walk around the street in front of where I staying, the Sask-Alta Rooms. She even bring some of her men in there, I think. That night I'm just lean on the wall between the rooming house and the Passtime Pool Hall watching people go by when she is stop by me and light up a cigarette.

"You want to go out?" she says.

"No, I live here for a while. I just standing around."

"I figure that but it don't do no harm to ask."

She is one pretty girl. She is Indian like me, full-blood I guess. She got her hair kind of curled up and a blond streak right across the front. She is wearing blue jeans real tight a faded jean jacket and a bright pink top under it that show most of the top of her breasts. She has a big leather purse over her shoulder.

"Where you from?" she ask me.

"Hobbema," I say. "That down past Wetaskiwin on the number two highway."

"I been by there. I used to live in Calgary for a while but I come from Saskatchewn. I'm Linda, Linda Star."

"I'm Silas Ermineskin," I tell her.

"If you're not doing anything why don't you buy me a beer," Linda say, and she smile at me real nice but real bold too, like she want something from me but she don't know how to ask.

These is sure fancy bars they got in the city. Where we go is called the New Ritz and it got pictures of the south seas all over the wall with girls in grass skirts shake themselves. The bar hold a couple of hundred or more people and they even got a band, Wanda and the Braves, which is Wanda, who is halfblood girl and one Indian guy on the drums and one guy on the steel guitar who is white but have a feather tied around his head.

"So what you doing in the big city?" Linda say to me.

I tell about how I taking a course on how to be a mechanic and have to come to NAIT, which is Northern Alberta Institute of Technology, for a course for three weeks. One that they don't have at Wetaskiwin where I go to school most of the time.

"I was never no good at school," she say. "I always run around too much and figure ways to get off that reserve. My father he used to beat

95

up me and my sister all the time and that ain't all he used to do either. Two years ago I run away with this guy from the oil rigs but he take off after a while and I start turning tricks." She give me her real bold smile like she daring me to say she ain't doing the right thing.

The band plays all the Hank Williams songs we like and Wanda she don't sing so good but she sing loud and Linda and me we dance some. She knows most everybody there and she keep go away and talk to people at other tables and especially to a thin-faced guy with reddy-blond hair that fall down over his face who sit with some black guys and a couple of white girls. Them guys is all dressed real fancy. The one Linda talks to is got on white pants and a black leather coat and wears a yellow wool scarf with purple fringes on it. I see her hand something to him once.

"Clifton over there is kind of my old man," say Linda. "We don't live together or nothing but he looks out for me if a trick gives me trouble and he take a real interest in me, you know what I mean. I give him some of my money and we get it on once in a while."

"Pretty girl like you must do a lot of business?" At first I not sure if I should talk about what she does or not but she sure don't mind at all.

"Never less than $100 a day. It pretty quiet tonight but I make lots of money this afternoon. You wait until the weekend, boy the street really swings. There are chicks going up and down checking all the parked cars. Some of the girls do their tricks in the cars but me I like a room. One Saturday I made over $200."

"Don't you ever get arrested?"

"I only been busted once in two years. Got a $50 fine and told I better go back to the reserve! Fat chance."

We dance some more when they play slow songs and kiss some on the dance floor.

"You ain't married or nothing are you?" Linda ask me.

"No."

"Not that it make any difference really it just that, I don't know, I don't even like to take a married trick. I do. But if I had an old man, I mean a real one, if I was married or something, I wouldn't want my guy messing around on me."

"I not married ... but I promised."

"They do that on your reserve too, eh? Guy named Billy Buckskin ask me when I thirteen. I'd still be sitting in that cabin waiting for him to decide if we should get married or not. I ain't got no time for that."

I think about my girlfriend Sadie One-wound back on the reserve and I know she's not mess around while I'm gone, and I don't feel right about what happening. But it don't take Linda long to make me forget about everybody but her.

"You gonna ask me back to your room, Silas?"

"Sure, but what about … " and I look over at the blond guy who is look back at me and I think wink his eye.

"I do anything I want anytime I want, okay? I pick up a half-dozen beers at the bar." Linda ain't let me buy even one glass of beer and I sure don't feel right about that either.

Boy, we sure do have one good time in my room. Linda sure is know about everything there is to know about make love. At least she know all I know and some more too. And she hold on to me like she been alone for a long time which I don't understand then.

She stay all night in my bed and when I get back from NAIT in the afternoon she still sleep there. When she see me she stretch and smile and say come hold her, and I do.

"I don't even go to work this afternoon," she say and laugh. "You have to kick my ass, Silas, or you never get me out of your bed."

That night we sit in the New Ritz beer parlour again and couple of times Linda go away for a while and come back show me twenty dollar bills under the table and she smile and be real proud of herself. So I smile with her.

She talk a lot with her blond friend whose name is Clifton Black and I sure figure they name him wrong and we laugh some about that. They is argue some and Linda is walk away from his table with her back straight and swing her bottom at him.

"I don't owe him nothing," she says, "and don't you be afraid of him either." I had never thought about be afraid of him before.

Linda and me spend a lot of time make love after that and we talk a lot about maybe what going to happen.

"My name ain't really Linda, you know. I changed it when I come to the city. I was called Lena before. Lena Starblanket. It funny we both got the family names of the reserve we come from. The Starblanket reserve really small, we hardly got any Indians at all there."

Then when we is hold each other real close in the night she is say to me, "Silas, I is like for us to get married ... or we could go back to where you live ... I don't think I would mind live on a reserve if I with you ... I go anywhere you want me to, Silas. I'd like to have your babies and I make you a good wife." I can't say she wouldn't and more and more I think what she say is a good idea.

Linda moves into my room. She don't have nothing to bring except another pair of jeans and a yellow sweater. "I got everything I own in my purse," she say and laugh. I can't help wonder where she spend all the money she make but I don't ask. Only I find out the next night in the New Ritz bar. Linda is away working and Clifton Black come sit at my table. His body move slow but his eyes is sure busy; they see everything goes on in the whole bar.

"I think it's time we have ourselves a talk, boy," he say to me, though I guess he no more that a year older than me. "You and Linda getting it on pretty heavy." I nod cause I don't know what else to do. I sure shaking inside cause by now I know what he carry a long knife in his boot and some even say he carry a gun too, and he supposed to be the best fist fighter on the street. He has three-four other girls give their money to him like Linda, and Linda is say he sell dope to a lot of people too. "I could get real tense about something like this," Clifton say. "Costs me a whole lot of bread every day that she's hung up on you, man." I like 'man' better than 'boy'.

"Linda don't take nothing that not her own," I say. "I look after Linda now so she don't need you no more." I think of myself as some brave to say something like that. I don't know what I would do if Linda did really need me help her with trouble. I not real strong or mean. Mostly not mean, I guess.

Clifton just keep on talking like he never heard me.

"I could probably whip you myself," he say eyeing me up and down, "but what I'll do, if I do, is bring along two or three friends and make dog food out of you. They'll be sewing you back together at the hospital for a month. I could do that ... but I ain't. You know why?"

I shake my head.

"Because that would make Linda go for you all the more. She'd feel responsible that you got hurt and it would give her a chance to play nurse. That's what these whores see themselves as, Silas, nurses and teachers and little old housewives. Did you know that?"

"We're kind of playing a game, Silas, you and me. I bet Linda's even talked about going back to the country with you." I know he can tell by look at my face that he's right. "How long do you figure that would last? She said anything to you about owning a chicken farm?"

"No."

"That's just a joke in the trade, boy. All whores are supposed to want to own chicken farms." And he laugh at me a little short laugh that sound like firecrackers go off. He got a few pimples on his face, and yellow fingers with a couple of big bright rings that I sure wish I had for my own.

"Linda came to the city to get away from a bad life and she's doing it the best way she knows how. And for her it is the best way. It's only natural that she should have some ideas about being somebody's wife and having kids and things like that. All whores get ideas in their heads like that once in a while. But it never works. You know why? Because they always pick themselves a nice straight guy to latch on to. A guy like you, Silas. You can no more live her life than she can live yours. I've seen it happen lots of times. Yes sir, we are playing a game, Silas, and old Clifton is a couple of points down right now but I got all the time in the world and I get real rough in the late going. I'm real glad we had this little talk, Silas, I just wanted you to know that Clifton he knows what's happening and though it might not seem like it now Clifton knows how to handle his girls."

I can't think of nothing to say to him.

"Hey, waiter," Clifton says, "bring my friend here a couple of beers." And he get up and walk away slow and casual so he show everybody in the bar he not worried by no Indian guy.

Linda is have surprise for me the next day when I come home. It is a suit like I seen in the stores downtown. It is jacket and pants blue like jeans but made from fancy cloth and cost maybe $75. There is a yellow shirt too and it sure make me happy.

"I should be buying you presents," I say.

"When you be a welder or whatever it is, then you buy for me. It make me proud to see you look good. I can say to everybody, that there's my old man, the one who looks so good."

I only got a couple of days before my course ends and I still not real sure what I going to do about Linda. I think I love her for sure, but I feel sad when I think of Sadie wait for me.

When I get back to my room, Linda is there but I sure surprised to see Clifton Black and a couple of young guys. I figure maybe Clifton decides I gonna be dog food after all.

"Hey, man," he says, "we didn't expect you back so soon. My friends here and I, we needed a nice quiet place to discuss some business," and he grins, does his little firecracker laugh and toss a little plastic package in his hand, "and Linda here let us use your room."

"I guess it okay," I say, and Clifton is grin and wink at me. His eyes is pale blue like a pail of skim milk. Then they start talk about money and dope and grams and stuff I don't understand much. Those young guys is from the university and they is making what they call a big buy of coke from Clifton so they can sell to all their friends.

They talk price for a while and they almost made their deal when all of a sudden the door bust open and three guys who look like bums and who I seen around the streets a few times, charge in waving guns and policeman badges. We all under arrest they say and start tear up the room look for dope.

As they come in I see Clifton hand Linda the little package and say stuff it. Linda reach down the front of her jeans and put it between her legs.

They line us four guys against the wall and search our clothes, then they tear up everything else in the room. They make us one by one, take off our clothes, and boy those guys sure look everywhere, even so they don't find nothing.

Then they turn to Linda. "Look," they say, "we followed Black here after he picked up the stuff. We could have nailed him but we wanted to catch him dealing. Now if you're holding you better cough it up and tell us who owns it."

The university guys is whine a lot about they don't know nothing. "Then how come you carrying $1500?" say one of the detectives. They can't answer and they shut up some after that.

"Well?" The detectives wait for Linda to say something.

"Tell them whose it is, Linda," I say to her.

"Hey, man," says Clifton, "be cool. Remember this is your room. You could have a lot of weight come down on you too. No sense in going to jail when she can. Just be cool, man. It'll all work out."

"Look, Miss," the biggest detective say to Linda, "we know you aren't dealing. All we want is the dope and we want to know who it belongs to. I'm sure you can clear up both points for us right now, and we'll let you walk out of here. But if we have to take you down to the police station and have a matron search you, and we find the dope then we're going to have to lay a charge against you — possession for trafficking is worth about five years."

"I – I have to think about it," says Linda. Clifton smiles at me showing a lot of crooked yellow teeth.

"Guess we all better go down to the station then," say the detectives.

Me and the university guys go in one car and Clifton and Linda each go in a separate one. Clifton he wink at Linda and blow her a kiss.

We all in one big room at the police station. There is just a long table, and chairs like you see in a school auditorium.

There is a policeman lady stand beside Linda.

"We'll give you one last chance," says the big detective. But Linda don't say nothing, so he nod to the lady policeman. She starts to take Linda out but just then Clifton is speak up.

"Hey, man. I can't let you bust my chick," he says. "I'll take my own weight. The stuff's mine." Then to Linda, "Give em the stuff, baby." And she does.

After a while they let us all go, except Clifton. But before I leave, Clifton he call me over to him.

"That was a really fine thing I did there, wasn't it, Silas?" He is grinning at me with everything but his eyes.

"You only done what you should have.

Linda don't do nothing wrong. It was your dope."

"There wasn't any dope, man."

"No?"

"There was nothing but bluff in that package. I was gonna burn them college kids. They wouldn't know dope if they were swimming in it, and what are they gonna do when they find out they've been burned ... go to the cops and say, 'Hey Mr. Policeman that bad dude Clifton Black burned me on a coke buy.'

"I could have cleared the air right away but I seen the chance to show you who Linda really belongs to. And I think you're smart enough to see it too.

"No sir, Linda came through for me just like I knew she would. My girls never let me down when it counts.

"She was standing there with what she thinks is a five-year bust for having my coke up her twat but she don't turn old Clifton in. When I train my girls I train them to stay. I hope you noticed that, boy."

"I noticed," I say.

"Don't feel bad. Whores are whores, Silas. I don't know what makes them that way. I just live and let live and take what comes my way. I know how to handle them and it ain't something you learn, it's something you're born with.

"Don't feel bad," he say again. "Old Clifton

106

he don't lose many. I'll surprise them all and be back on the street tomorrow. I just have to wait until they send the stuff out to be analysed. Nothing but bluff, man, nothing but bluff. Be cool, and I'll see you around," he says, and offers to shake hands. Only he got to shake hands that funny way that his black friends must of taught him like we going to arm wrestle.

We walking back from the police station to the Sask-Alta Rooms.

"I think I gonna find myself another place to stay," I say.

"Silas, I thought everything is okay now. Neither of us in any trouble. Guess you mad cause I let them guys in the room. I'm sorry, Silas. I don't do that again."

"It a lot more than that, Linda."

"Silas, stay and be my old man. You don't have to work or nothing. Or you can keep on going to school or whatever you want. We can get an apartment, or even rent a house. I make lots of money. And Silas, we can buy a car. I'll buy you a car. And we can love lots. God, I love it so when you hold me, and you get off on me too, I know you do. Clifton he won't bother us none. He be in jail for a while but even when he gets back he won't. He could of let me go to jail today but he didn't. Silas, what I try to tell you is I love you and I don't want to be alone."

"You don't even know what you done back

there, do you?"

"I didn't do anything."

"Yes you did. You had to make a choice between me and Clifton and you chose him."

"How... "

"You know that dope was his but still you let yourself go to jail for him."

"But I didn't. It all worked out okay."

"Not for me."

"But I do love you, Silas." What I want to tell her then is: yes, you love me, but not enough to put me first. But I don't. "I don't mean what I did to hurt you. You don't under-stand...."

"I understand enough to know you never gonna be Lena Starblanket no more. You always gonna be Linda Star and you always gonna live right here or on some other street like this." I think that maybe if I don't have Sadie One-wound wait for me at home I give it a try here but I just got too much to lose.

"You could be wrong, Silas. Maybe I could be Lena Starblanket again, with the right guy."

I take a deep breath. "I leave the key with the manager. The room is paid up for two more days."

Linda is give me kind of a sad smile. "I think I'll stop off at the New Ritz, have a beer and see what happening."

We stop together in front of the hotel.

"Silas," she say to me, and she use that kind

of smile like the first time I met her. "If you ever in town and you feel like … you know … you never have to pay me."

She is walk up the single step to the door of the New Ritz beer parlour, give her bottom a real nice wiggle at me, then she go in and the door close slow behind her.

The Kid in the Stove

"Tell us a story, Silas," the kids say to me a lot of evenings. I tell them lots of stories about our legends of how the Great Spirit made the land and us, and even a few that I made up myself. But no matter how many I tell, just about when it be time for bed they say, "Tell us about the kid in the stove."

For that one they all gather around close to me. Minnie and Thomas, Delores and Hiram, my little brothers and sisters. And there is Joseph too, my big brother. He is 22 already, but when he just a baby he catch the scarlet fever and his mind is never grow up like his body do. Joseph, he talk like the wind-up record player when it not cranked up good enough. "I ... be ... the ... kid ... that ... hid ... in ... the ... stove ... " and he grin and shake, happy a little, like a dog that know he gonna be petted.

So I tell them the story. Ma, she used to tell it to me and Illianna and Joseph when we was little, and she say her mother used to

110

tell it to her. It kind of our own private scary story about how Lazarus Bobtail and all but one of his kids was murdered by a white man named Donald Henry Ditesman. It happened a long time ago when there was hardly any town at Wetaskiwin, and the reserve here at Hobbema was new. Mrs. Bobtail was away someplace is how come she didn't die too. Afterward, they say she married with a Blood Indian from down south, moved away and nobody ever heard of her or the kid in the stove no more.

I don't know why kids like scary stories but they sure do. I make everybody be quiet and turn the lamp down low and then I tell about this crazy white man come creep around the Bobtail cabin, peek in the window and try the door real careful.

"You guys think you hear anything?" I say. And they always do. They move in closer to me, and Delores, the littlest one, hold on to Joseph's neck real tight. Then I finish the story about how that Ditesman guy is shoot Lazarus Bobtail and four of his kids, but how the fifth kid crawl right up inside the big old cookstove in the cabin, and he get to live to tell all about it.

Once, some of us went up to the spot where them children died, and it make us feel all creepy. It ain't on the reserve no more: the Government, it take away land whenever it feel like it, and our reserve get smaller as it get older. The place was lonely even in the daytime. All we could find was a few logs people say was part of Lazarus Bobtail's cabin. Just being there at the place where it really happen make us think a lot about the story. I remember how when I first hear it, I figure that if something like that ever happened at our place, I'd of been the smart kid that hid in the stove and got to live. And I bet everybody who hear it think the same way.

For such a sad story it almost make a happy ending when you hear at the end that one child got away. Most anybody in these parts, Indian or white, can tell you about that escape. They're real certain about it, as certain as they are that we live on the Ermineskin Reserve and that the town down at the highway is called Hobbema. Yet it never happen at all.

I like to know about Indian history in Alberta, and I've read the couple of books in the Wetaskiwin library that are about Indians, maybe three-four times. I get to thinking about how I would like to know the history-book story of the Bobtail Massacre.

Mr. Nichols, my English instructor down at the Tech School in Wetaskiwin, the guy who is fix up the spelling in my stories, says maybe I could find out from the RCMP or maybe from the Glenbow Foundation in Calgary, who are people keep records of Indian history in Alberta.

The RCMP guys don't help much. They all

young guys and I think they come maybe from places where they don't have no Indians. They make fun on me when I ask, want to know where my tomahawk, and how come an Indian kid like me want to be bothered worry about something that happen so long ago. They say maybe they get what I want for me if I tell them who's got a still on the reserve and where it's at. So I go away.

Next time I go to Calgary, I leave my girl-friend Sadie One-wound look around in the Goodwill Store while I take the bus out to the Glenbow place. I meet with a real nice man called Mr. Hugh Dempsey. He is white but he got Indian wife, and and he have a picture of her right up on his desk to show he not ashamed to have her. He talk soft on me and make me feel calm, cause I sure not used to big fancy buildings and people run around all dressed up all the time.

Mr. Dempsey is look in his books and things and he give me a paper to read and I copy some of it down.

On the night of July 14, 1907, an itiner-ant railroad worker named Donald Henry Deutchmann had a dispute, in the town of Wetaskiwin, with some Indians from the Ermineskin Reserve which is located at Hobbema, some eleven miles distant. The nature of the dispute is not clear, but late that night, Deutchmann apparently walked from Wetaskiwin to the reserve, stopped at the first Indian residence that he came to, that of Lazarus Bobtail, entered and shot to death Bobtail and his four children. The bodies were discovered the next day by Bobtail's wife, White Sky. Deutchmann was arrested the same day by the Mounties, but was judged insane and the case never came to trial.

Mr. Dempsey he find me another book with a little chapter about Deutchmann, but the story is the same, not near as scary down in history as when told at night in a cabin with a coal-oil lamp make shadow all over.

I feel kind of sad that there ain't nothing nowhere about the kid that got away. When I ask Mr. Dempsey about it he say that maybe part of the story is taken from some other story that happened here or maybe someplace else. He say that lots of times people get things mixed up like that when a story been told for a lot of years like that one has.

Mr. Dempsey, he point out another little paragraph in the book and say that maybe it explains a whole lot. That paragraph is say that a month or so after the murders, before Mrs. Bobtail move away, she is have a baby. Just a baby, the book don't say if it was a boy or a girl.

I think about that real hard, and when I hear

Mr. Dempsey explain it, I have to agree with him. I know when I was little and hear the story, when they get to the part where everybody been shot, I always ask, "And did all the children die?" and I know the kids I tell the story to do the same.

What Mr. Dempsey suggest is that, way back, somebody, in the way big people like to make fun on kids and make a joke for themselves at the same time, say, "They all died but the one in the oven." Everybody growed up knows that that's a way for saying a lady is gonna have a baby.

Saying that would make the kids feel better about a sad story, and the big people could laugh and wink their eyes at each other. It seem to me that that is likely the way it happened and little by little the story got changed over the years until everybody is believe there really was a kid in the stove.

Boy, I can hardly wait to get back and tell everybody what I found out. All these years everybody is have the story all wrong, but, boy, I sure gonna fix that up in a hurry. I guess we going to have to get us a new scary story to tell, cause it is the kid in the stove part that make the Bobtail Massacre not just another murder story.

I feel kind of tingly all over and I'm almost as excited as the time I knew I was going to Edmonton to buy my new pair of cowboy boots. Yet when I meet with Sadie, I tell her don't bother me about what I found out at Glenbow.

On the bus on the way home I start to think about how much I liked that story, and how the kids I tell it to sure get a bang out of it.

Sadie want to talk to me but I tell her I got something to think about. She say maybe she wishes she was going to marry a bronc-buster like Eathen Firstrider intead of a guy like me, who sneak around all the time write down what people say. Finally, she just run her knee up against mine and look at her Country Music Song Book that she bought in Calgary with a picture of Donna Fargo on the cover.

That story like we been telling it, is not really the truth, but it sure make a lot of kids happy for a lot of years, and I wonder who it gonna make feel good, besides me, if I tell what I found out. It seem to me that it kind of like … well, the reasons you don't shoot songbirds is that they don't do nobody no harm.

I look sideways at Sadie, and she look at me and then she put her head on my shoulder. I reach down and put my hand on the leg of her jeans.

"You finished thinking, Silas?" she asks.

"Yeah," I say.

Ups and Downs

"And the winner is ... Silas Ermineskin!"

Only the man read it, "Silas ... Ermine-skin??"

I bet you could hear the groan that went up from the Canadian Legion hall, not just across the street to the Gold Nugget Café, but all the way down the block to the Alice Hotel.

I never intend to be there for the drawing. I just on my way out of town from visit my girlfriend Sadie One-wound at the hospital where she have her appendix out a couple of days before. The Lions Club bingo is almost over and I hang around the door see if I can get a ride back to the reserve with somebody.

What I win is the Wetaskiwin Lions Club Ladies' Auxiliary Trip For Two To Fabulous Las Vegas. A month or so ago me and Sadie was walk around the shopping centre and I buy a ticket for 25 cents and promise Sadie I win for sure.

I wait until most everybody gone home before I go up and show the guy my ticket and

117

my ID from the Tech school and collect what I won. I figure then that me and Sadie will go when she get better but the guy tell me that the tickets is for a charter flight day after tomorrow and I got to go then or never.

If I can't take Sadie, then I figure I take Ma, but when I tell her she just laugh and say no way she gonna fly on them big iron birds. She really say that. In our language there was no word for airplane until the airplane come around and the word we call them is mean iron bird.

That leaves me either go alone or take my friend Frank Fence-post.

Part of the deal that go with win the tickets is the Lions Club Junior Young People's Band is come toot their horns and stuff to wish the winners goodbye. They is usually play for somebody they all know, like somebody who belong to the Lions Club or one of the big farmers around Wetaskiwin, and everybody is have a good time.

We is the first Indians ever win that trip and some of the losers is still groaning when we is leave real early in the morning from the Wetaskiwin bus depot to ride to Calgary to catch our airplane. There are only five or six of the band there and they all look sleepy and their uniforms ain't done up so good. They play a little bit of Kawliga, and something somebody say is Indian Love Call. Then the Mayor of

Wetaskiwin, Mr. J. William Oberholtzer, who ain't shaved this morning, shake hands on Frank and me and tells us have a good trip.

I don't find out for quite a few months but what usually goes with the prize is a hotel room to stay in and $500 to spend. But since the ticket is just say a trip to two, that's what we get, a trip for two. Me and Frank got maybe $20 each in money and we sure don't know what to expect in Las Vegas, or even for sure where, or what Las Vegas is.

I borrow me Eathen Firstrider's buckskin jacket with the coloured beads all over the back and fringes on the sleeves, and I got on my cherry-coloured western shirt with about 50 pearl buttons down the front.

At the airport in Calgary the airplane guy wants to check our luggage. He is dressed in red blazer, look like he got a smile painted on his face and got his hair oiled pretty nice.

"We ain't got any suitcases," I tell him.

"Indeed," he says, and lifts one eyebrow about half an inch. "Aren't you planning on changing your clothes?"

"Why?" asks Frank. "We only gonna be gone two weeks."

The airplane ride is pretty good. We is hardly scared at all once we get up in the air. The airplane we is on is chartered by the Camrose Lutheran College Choir, who is going to sing at some big convention or something.

Lutherans don't drink or smoke, or do much of nothing, so all they serve to drink on the plane is milk and stuff.

The Lutherans, they is all figure we on the wrong plane until we tell them we is the winners of the Wetaskiwin Lions Club Ladies Auxiliary Trip For Two To Fabulous Las Vegas. After that, they pretend we not there and practise sing their hymns.

"Hey, partner," Frank says to me. "One good thing about have all these Lutherans sing songs around us is that this plane don't dare crash. I figure if it start to go down they just pray it right back up again."

We do have one bottle of Sam Standing-at-the-door's dandelion wine and it ain't so bad mixed with milk.

Boy, that Las Vegas is the hottest place I ever been in my life. It feel like we walk right into an oven when we get off the plane.

"This here must be the Sahara Desert," says Frank taking off his red checkered mackinaw right quick. The choir got a couple of buses wait for them at the airport, but nobody offers us a ride so we take a taxi.

"Where to?" says the driver.

"Las Vegas," I tell him.

"It's a big place, Mac."

"Take us where the action is," say Frank.

I seen a big sign at the airport say, Come To Caesar's Palace, so I tell the driver take us there.

"You sure you guys got money?" the driver wants to know.

We have a good laugh about that cause cab drivers in Edmonton and Calgary ask us the same thing. The cab costs us eight dollars.

We go into Caesar's Palace. Boy, that Caesar must be some rich dude. It about as big as the whole town of Hobbema, air-conditioned, covered in carpet and smell like the inside of a new car.

"We like to get a room, please," I tell the pretty man behind the desk, who got long blond hair look like it been mixed with glue.

"That will be $47," he say, and curl up his lip like a dog growl at a stranger.

"That for one week or two?" Frank ask, as we both count out our money on the counter.

"That for one night. Check-out time is 11.00 am."

We only got $29 between us both.

"I stay for a whole week at the Sask-Alta Rooms in Edmonton for $21," I tell the clerk.

"I'm sure you did," he say, and his nose flare out like a horse when he speak on us.

After we have steaks and a few beers there ain't much left of the $29.

Maybe we can get a job or something, I think. Me and Frank been to the Tech School at Wetaskiwin over a year now, learn about how to fix tractors.

We get real tired so we crawl in the back

seat of somebody's car, sleep for a while, and it getting daylight before they come along yell at us to get out or they call the police.

We see a sign say "69-cent breakfast," and we have a couple of them each. Then we walk through the casino look at the games and slot machines. The part I like best though is the washroom. They is all mirrors and white marble and they got free hair stuff and perfume. Me and Frank is sure smell good when we through in there.

About the second time I put a nickel in a slot machine I win two-fifty. This look like a pretty good thing. Frank take a bunch of nickels and get two machines go at once, and sure enough he win twenty dollars after a while.

"I like to play me some of these other games," say Frank, but when he tries to put a handful of nickels on the big green table, the guy with the stick tell him he got to buy chips from someplace. When he goes to do that I just stand around some watch the old white ladies in bright dresses poke in their nickels in the slot machines. When I see one put in money for a long time and not win nothing, I put in maybe ten nickels after she changes machines. I don't make a lot of money but I sure don't lose any and my pockets is get heavy with all that silver.

Then I see Frank over by the big green table. He is stand at one side by himself and every-body is go ooh and ahh.

"Hey, Silas, I put down five chips on one of them squares and my money is get bigger and bigger." I look over the edge and there is three tall piles of chips. Everybody goes ooh again real loud and the man put down lots more chips.

There is a black man stand beside us. He look Frank up and down and say, "You ought to pick up your chips, son, your luck can't hold out forever."

"You mean I can pick them up?" says Frank. "I thought I had to wait until they ready to pay me. You pick it up for me, mister, I afraid I touch something I shouldn't."

We thank that black fellow a lot and we each got our pockets and hands full of chips. We take them off to cash them and boy we got almost $1000. Neither me or Frank ever seen so much money before.

We go back to Caesar's Palace and I tell that dude on the desk, "We have us a room for three nights and if it ain't fancy enough for us here we go someplace else."

"I'm sure you will find everything satisfactory, Mr. Ermineskin," he say, and I can see all the way up his nose when he say it. "Perhaps you would care for one of our suites? They are priced from $150 per day."

"Why not?" says Frank. "We rich Indians now."

There is room for four or five families in the

suite they give us. We sure wish we have some friends there we could invite in.

We have a big dinner and lots of drinks and we take taxis all over Las Vegas. I buy me a pair of hand-tooled purple cowboy boots and I buy Sadie a pair just like mine only for lady cowboys.

The last taxi driver hear us talk about how rich we are and ask if maybe we like to have some girls for company, and we say sure.

The girls come up to our room after a while. They is big tall white girls. They is some pretty but the one that's mine I sure have trouble talking to. We don't understand each other much. She talks like that Gomer Pyle fellow I seen on TV but she tell me that I talk funny.

Them girls want $100 each and then they make us have a bath and wash us all over real good before they let us mess around with them. And Frank's girl, who called Candy, keep calling up on the phone to someplace called Room Service and orders us up drinks and steaks and wine and stuff. She ain't very friendly to Frank at all until we is start to mess around. Then I hear her say to Frank, "Now I know why you're called Fence-post," and she giggle real pretty.

After that she make a lot of noises like she having a good time.

We all go to sleep after while and when we wake up in the morning the girls is gone and so is what money Frank and me had left. What make me really mad though is they steal them new cowboy boots that I bought for Sadie.

I don't tell Frank right then but I put a $50 bill in the toe of my new boots and it is still there. So we gonna be okay for a while. We call up that Room Service place and order some more steak and wine for breakfast. It sure is nice of the hotel to send up all this stuff whenever we ask.

We just lay around all day, then I tell Frank my surprise and we call up a taxi take us downtown so we can make some more party. I tell the taxi driver wait for me while I go in a bar get some change.

I give the guy my $50 bill and he give me back four quarters.

"Where the rest of it?" I ask him.

"What rest? You give me a buck, I give you four quarters."

"I gave you $50," I yell. It is a dark little bar and there is five or six guys sit along on stools but don't say nothing.

"Get out of here," say the bartender, "and don't be trying to pull that old rip-off on me."

"But I ... " but then a couple of big guys get up off the bar stools. They is a lot bigger than me, they is bigger than both Frank and me.

"Get out of here, kid," they say, "or we chop you up for dog meat."

I sure feel like crying, maybe, but I go like

they say. Outside, I open the door of the taxi and yell, "Run Frank." We both do, but boy that taxi guy is quick. He drive up on the sidewalk and almost hit us except the door I left open smash on a parking meter and he have to stop.

We finally walk back to the hotel. In the morning that guy on the desk catch us as we walk by say he want to see some money for all the room service we used. We can't talk him into waiting none so we have to run again, cause the room service bill is even bigger than the one more day we got paid up.

All we got left is some silver money so we go down to a casino and hang round the slot machines see if anybody forget to pick up some change. First we try to win some money again but we lost everything we had. Then a man come up to us, take us each by an arm and say it time for us to leave. The guy look like one of them professional wrestlers I seen in Calgary once: no neck and chest like a barrel. He got a tag on his suitpocket say, "Security." He is pull Frank and me toward the door when a man look like that TV doctor Marcus Welby step up and say in a deep voice like a radio announcer, "May I have a word with you, Fowler?"

He take the guard off to one side but I can hear him.

"I want you to check those boys very thoroughly before you remove them. Last week you threw out that young fellow who was wearing only a pair of purple velvet tennis shorts, well it seems that he was a famous rock musician and he went across to the Flamingo and dropped $40,000 playing baccarat. Just be sure these boys aren't in the same category."

"You guys belong to a band?" the security guy say to us.

"Ermineskin," we answer together.

"Where are you playing?"

"Caesar's Palace," I say.

"The Desert Inn," says Frank.

"Caesar's Palace first, then the Desert Inn," I explain. "We gonna be here two weeks."

"Ahh-haaw," say the man with the deep voice. "Gentlemen, I want you to feel welcome here. My name is John Wendell and if you ever need anything at all, feel free to ask my assistance." He put one hand over his head and snap his fingers and a girl in a short skirt appear with a tray of drinks. I take one. Frank takes two.

"We sort of left our money at the hotel," I say. "Maybe you could borrow us a twenty or so."

"What hotel are you staying at?"

"Caesar's Palace." He nod to Fowler who disappear real fast.

"And how long have you gentlemen been musicians?"

"Not very long," say Frank. And that sure the truth. Sometimes after I have quite a few beers I sing Take These Chains From My Heart. Sadie get mad and punch me on the shoulder cause she think I sing it to her personal. I can't play no music and Frank he blow on the mouth organ sometimes, scare away the dogs from in front of the cabin.

Fowler come back in a minute.

"They got a suite at Caesar's," he say to Mr. Wendell. "Sure could have fooled me." He could have fooled me too, but I guess Mr. Caesar still think we staying at his place.

"Gentlemen," Mr. Wendell say with his arm around our shoulders, "Would, say, $10,000 credit be sufficient?" When I don't answer right away he raise it to $20,000 and add, each, to it.

I'd sooner he gave us maybe $100 cash. Frank and me don't win money no more when we play the tables and things. In fact I think we lost quite a bit. What we do get is all the food and drinks we want and we get a front-row seat to see Merle Haggard in their big dining room. We sure stomp and clap our hands for him. It not just that Merle Haggard is a good singer, everybody know that he been in jail and it make him seem more like a real person.

All our credit ain't no good when it comes night cause they figure we live and work at Caesar's Palace. We get chased out of a couple of parked cars so we sleep out on the Desert Inn Golf Course with our jackets wrapped around us.

Early in the morning we creep up to a swimming pool behind one of the big motels. We peek through the hedge and see two guys about fifty is swim around some.

"We just wash a little in the low end of the pool," say Frank.

"You think those guys will mind? We don't want no trouble."

"They must be a hundred feet away. There's lots of room." So we take off all our clothes but our shorts and start step in the low water. I never seen guys move so fast as them two. They pull themselves out of the pool so quick they take about half the water with them.

"What are you guys doing here?" they yell at us.

"We is just going to wash ourselves a little. We don't mean to scare you," I say.

"This here hotel's reserved for the Brotherhood of Clans Convention," the one with the reddest face says.

"Well you just go on swimming," says Frank. "We try not to bother you none."

They both got red faces, big bellies and beady eyes. They look like a lot of the farmers around Wetaskiwin.

"You guys some of them wetbacks?"

"We Cree Indians, from Canada," I tell them.

"Yer injuns, eh? By God, I never seen an

injun close up before. We don't have none out our way. Got coons though. Thousands of coons. They's a lot blacker than you."

Frank and me start to put our clothes on.

"We sorry we disturb you," I say.

"Y'all talk like you got a mouthful of grits, boy."

"Hey, Buford," says one to the other, "you hear what they called the coon who married an injun. A social climber." They both have a good laugh about that. Frank and me we go down and sneak in the washroom at a Phillips 66 station and wash our face and hands.

We just hang around town all day and sleep on the golf course again that night.

We is sure broke and now we is getting hungry too. Yesterday I pawned Eathen Firstrider's buckskin jacket for five dollars, but we spend that already for food and cigarettes.

"I sure wish we could go home now," I say.

"Silas, we got the tickets," say Frank, jumping up and down.

I got the airplane tickets folded up careful in the back pocket of my jeans.

"We can't sell them," I say, "or maybe we never get home again."

"You got a driver's license, Silas. We borrow some money on the tickets, rent us a car, then we be a taxi for a while, and make lots of money. We pay for the car and have enough left for some food and a good time."

It sound like not too bad an idea to me. There is sure a lot of taxis around and mostly they got people in them.

Trouble is, the places that rent cars run us off every time. They all got pretty girls dressed up fancy who smile and is friendly until they find out we got no real money. Then they wrinkle up their noses and tell us go away. We about to give up that idea when we see a place — Easy Ralph's Used Car Rentals and Dating Service — marriages performed 24 hours a day.

The windows is so dirty we can hardly see in. There is a fat guy with a brush cut sit behind a little desk and smoke a cigar

"You Mr. Easy Ralph?" I ask.

"Maybe, maybe not," he say.

"We like to rent one of your premium unit used cars," Frank says.

"Then I'm Easy Ralph," say the man, and he stand up and shake hands on me and Frank.

He don't much like the idea of us only have our plane tickets for money, but we promise him we left our money at our hotel and we pay him for sure when we bring the car back.

"I guess you guys can't go too far without your tickets, eh?" says Easy Ralph. He slap our back and rent us a 1965 Rambler station wagon with only one fender bashed in.

We have pretty good luck be a taxi, for a while. We just drive up and down the strip, look for people look like they need a ride. I stop and Frank jump out and open the back door like we seen real taxi drivers do, and say, "Taxi."

Everybody want to know how come we ain't got a meter. We tell them it okay, we trust them to pay us what is fair. And most of them do, I think. Lucky most of them just want to go from one hotel to another. Frank, he look out the window for hotel signs and I watch the road. We only go the wrong way maybe twice. We made about $30 when a real taxi driver chase us out from in front of the Sands Hotel and pretty soon a police car is pull us over. We tell him it ain't us that's a taxi, must be somebody look like us.

The policeman smile and say he reckon there ain't anybody else in Las Vegas look like us. He tell me that both me and the car need about ten licenses to be a taxi and we better not take no more passengers or he run us in.

We park the car and go in quite a few bars. We end up at one with a big sign say now appearing Stark Naked and The Car Thieves. Stark Naked is. The Car Thieves play music while she take off her clothes. We is have a few drinks, about $30 worth.

"Remember downtown, Silas, we seen that wooden Indian in front of that store? I figure, tomorrow, I try and rent you to that store man. He probably pay plenty have a real Indian stand out front all day."

We have a real good laugh about that, but I guess we laugh too loud cause a big guy in a black suit ask us we should leave.

"Hey, Partner! How'd you like to rent my friend," says Frank. "He's a real Indian."

The guy in the suit shove us so hard out the door we'd of gone right in the street if we hadn't hit up against a parked car. Frank does a bit of a war dance on the curb, and tell that guy he put a curse on him. "You gonna bleed to death the next time you take a piss," he tell him, but the guy don't look worried.

Frank say he gonna drive, and I say okay but be careful. Frank he drove Eathen's car around the reserve some but he never been on a real road before.

I dozed off for a while and wake up with a big bang and it raining in my window. I don't know how Frank done it and I guess he don't either, but he nosed the car right up against one of them statues outside of Caesar's Palace

There is lots of people stand around look at us. Frank, he peel himself off the steering wheel. "I don't think Mr. Easy Ralph gonna like this."

I don't guess anybody like it very much. My head sure hurts where it hit the windshield. The water is run in the door now and there is a wet white lady with one arm busted clean off staring at me from the middle of the pool.

In the rear view I see the red light of a police car come race along the road. "I think we should get to someplace else real fast, Partner," I tell Frank.

Everybody is yell, "There they go," and, "Stop them Indians," as me and Frank run across the road and behind some buildings. I think they shot at us, but I don't stop to ask anybody for sure.

We sleep on the golf course that night and next morning we start for out of town. At Caesar's there is nothing but that busted white lady to show that we ever been there.

We walk toward the end of town. It is some hot on my bare feet and I sure wish I hadn't lost my boots someplace last night. We hitch-hike on the edge of the road for a long time but the cars all go by like they don't even see us.

"I wonder how far it is to Hobbema?" say Frank, wiping the sweat off his forehead with his sleeve.

"I wonder which way it is for sure," I answer him.

Penance

Last summer during the pilgrimage to Lac Ste.-Anne, Annie Bottle is walk five miles up the old railroad grade in her bare feet to give thanks for something. It hard to figure what it might be. Annie got eight kids that always hungry and the meanest drunk husband on the reserve.

Fred Bottle is one bad dude. He drink up the Welfare cheque as soon as it come, and he beat up Annie and the kids whenever the spirit move him.

I'm nineteen, and Annie, for all them kids, ain't that much older than me. She was one of the Stonechild girls and married Fred Bottle when she is about fifteen. Figure a kid a year for eight years or so, and that make her maybe 25, but she look 40, or worse. Ma, she sends us over with food for them sometimes and Mad Etta do all their doctoring. Sometimes when Fred Bottle is in jail everything be pretty good for a while, but he always come back.

Annie is pretty small and skinny, and she wears long skirts and a flowered kerchief like the old ladies do. She is always walk like she climbing a hill and is all the time look at the ground.

I been to Lac Ste.-Anne a couple of times before, when I was little, but this is the first time since I growed up. Boy, it is some busy place. They say there is over 10,000 Indians come here this week. Me and Frank Fence-post is come down with Rufus Firstrider. Rufus, he want to look things over. He got this white girl that he really love, but she been pretty sick for a long time now, and he figure mabe if he dip her in the lake, Ste. Anne make a miracle and she won't be sick no more.

Ste. Anne, they say is the Virgin Mary's mother, and they say that a long time ago some people seen her here at this lake. I sure don't know what she would be doing way out here in Alberta at a lake that got so many black flies and mosquitoes, when she could be someplace nice. I figure that saints, they can go just about any place they want to. Ever since she was seen here, every summer, Indian peoples is come from all over the province to dip themselves in Lac Ste.-Anne and make themselves better of whatever makes them sick.

I never seen so many Indians in one place before, not even at the Calgary Stampede. Tree to tree Indians, is what Frank say we got here. There is crowds all along the beach so you can hardly walk. All the campgrounds is full and people is make tents all over the place. Down to the bar in the Lac Ste.-Anne Hotel they have taken out all the tables and chairs and everybody is sit on the floor so they can get more people in the bar. Also they know what happen in other years is that the tables and chairs get all busted up if they is left there.

There is guys in little trailers sell hot dogs and pop, and other ones that sell candy fluff, and one big one that sell religious medals and pillows of dark blue silk with a big face of Jesus in red beads.

They even got a couple of search lights that light up the sky at night, and I hear that on Sunday the Air Force gonna do some trick flying over the lake. Somebody say that there is gonna be church services someplace, but we never find any.

What we do find is a booth that is rent out trail bikes, and boy we sure do agree that we would like to have some. I'm the only one who got a driver's license, so I go and rent one, give it to Frank, go back, rent another, give it to Rufus, and finally rent one for me.

"Haven't I seen you before?" the guy say to me the last time.

"Not me," I say. "All us Indians look alike."

We make those trail bikes roar real loud and backfire some and we sure is happy. We scatter people out of the way and find us this old raiload grade to ride on. We ride out for a couple of miles or so. Frank, he like to slide down the banks, run through water, and shoot mud out behind the bike.

We come to a spot where there used to be a bridge in the grade but it is fall down a long time ago. There is a little water under it and you can smell the tar-stuff that the timbers been dipped in. Frank pretend he is this Evel Knievel fellow and he gonna jump right over that hole in the road.

If it hadn't been that Frank's bike only go about half way across where the bridge used to be, and he tip right over backward and fall into the long grass and the water, we wouldn't have found Annie Bottle.

Annie, she big with her next baby, and I guess she got tired with walking and rest for a while on side of the grade in the tall grass. It is while she rest there that the baby start to come and she get sick. We hear her groan some, and she about as surprised to see us as we are to see her.

First she tell us go away, she don't want nobody help her. Then she have some more pains and she say maybe it okay if we do something. Annie is hold on with both hands to a poplar branch she pulled off a tree. Her fist is white and the branch bent up in a half circle. But we is just stand around for a while. We sure don't know what to do with a lady gonna have a baby, maybe right away.

The sun is hot and there is lots of little flies buzz around. Annie say she thirsty but we don't have nothing to drink with us, and we sure don't think she should drink that green water from the slough. We lie her down in the shade and take off her shoes, tell her try not to have the baby for a while.

We decide Rufus he should stay with Annie cause he got lots training look after a sick people. Me and Frank we go call at a farm we seen back across a meadow a ways, see if we can use the phone to call somebody. The farmer he look us up and down and say he ain't got no phone, even though the telephone poles run right into his yard. We ask if maybe there is a hospital around someplace, but he say Stony Plain is the closest and that is maybe 40 miles.

We go back across to where Rufus and Annie is. We try to get her to walk some, but she is hardly able. We try to sit her on the back of my bike but that don't work either. With Frank and Rufus hold one arm each we get her down the road maybe a mile toward Lac Ste.-Anne when we see some buildings back off the grade aways, look like nobody lives in them. There ain't no house but there is quite a few buildings, and there is haystacks in the yard. We pick out a nice shed and with the hay make Annie a good place to lie down.

We talk it over for a while and decide that I should go to Lac Ste.-Anne, find Mad Etta.

First place I try is the hotel, and there is Mad Etta sit in the middle the beer parlour floor, smoke a big fat roll-yer-own, and drink beer. When Etta go out there is room for three people come in. It take me and a couple of guys just to get her up on her feet. Etta I bet cure as many people as Ste. Anne if they was to have a contest.

"Etta not used to sit on the floor," she say, and laugh and laugh. I sure not laugh much. I got to figure how to get Etta back to that farm. It is pretty hard to get a 300-pound lady on the seat of a trail bike. Etta take up the whole seat and her big belly keep pushing me right up against the handlebars. The bike keep stalling too cause it ain't used to carry so much weight. I sure wish we had Louis Coyote's pickup truck so we could load Mad Etta in the back the way we do at home when we want to take her someplace.

We go along the grade about 50 feet at a time, but I just keep starting the bike again and again cause I know that once I get Etta there everything gonna be okay cause Etta be better any day than those white-man doctors.

Frank and Rufus is sure glad to see us. Annie is cry some and say that the baby is come soon. Etta tell us a list of things she needs for Annie and the baby, and away the three of us go on our bikes.

The Lac Ste.-Anne store is sold out of most

everything but warm pop, Frito chips and cigarettes, and none of that stuff is on Mad Etta's list. We stop at the hotel, pick up a box of beer for Annie and Etta to drink, then we got to ride back past where we come from to get to the next town.

From the farm we have to drive across a field to the main road and about ten miles to a store. We get most of the stuff Mad Etta wants, like a saucepan so she can cook up her medicine. I bet Etta is out dig up roots, pick leaves and stuff, right now. We get some bandage, some iodine, and some diapers come in a big box, a couple of blankets, some spray keep mosquitoes away, a loaf of bread, some margarine, a couple of pounds bologna, and a carton of cigarettes. They even cash my unemployment cheque without too much hassle.

"Maybe we should buy something for the baby," say Frank.

We go back in get a bottle of pop each and some ice cream on a stick, then I buy a rattle that is pink on one side and blue on the other, Frank get a doll with red hair and big round eyes, and Rufus get a giant economy size can of Johnson's Baby Powder.

Then we start back for the farm. It is already dark and we not so sure which way we come from, but we just look up at the sky and see the searchlights at Lac Ste.-Anne and we follow them right to where we going.

Mad Etta got a little fire going in the ground. She torn most of one side out of her five-flour-sack dress, and that is what the baby is wrapped up in.

Annie Bottle is lay in the hay in the shed with the baby at her chest.

"It's a girl," Mad Etta tells us. "Annie, she be okay. She's tough. But I not so sure about the baby."

The baby, her face is all screwed up in a scowl, and the fire reflect in her little black eyes. She look like a turnip been all winter in the root cellar.

We is give Annie the presents we bought for the baby. She even smile a little before her and the baby go to sleep.

The four of us sit around the little fire for a while.

"Why do you guys figure she was walk alone way out here?" Mad Etta is say to us. But me, or nobody else, got any answers.

Us guys go sleep in a haystack. Mad Etta keep the fire go all night, cook up some stuff from roots and leaves that she feed by little drops to the baby.

Couple of times the next day we is go to town buy more stuff for Mad Etta and the baby. Annie Bottle is up and walk around some, but the baby cry most of the time in a tiny, dry voice.

"I can't figure why that baby don't get

stronger," Mad Etta say that night. "Etta look after babies in worse place than this and they don't die," and she tip up her bottle of Lethbridge Pale Ale, and in the firelight, the bottle and her face is the same colour.

Sometime about sunup, the baby, she is die.

We don't have a shovel or nothing. We just scoop out a little grave in the soft ground.

"She sure is one tiny thing," say Frank, as he carry her out of the shed wrapped up in a green-and-plaid blanket. "She light as a bird."

We bury the baby, her toys and everything. Then we cover up the spot good with rocks in case animals come around.

"Only one good thing," say Rufus, "is it be one less kid for Fred Bottle to beat around."

We agree among ourselves that we ain't gonna tell nobody about what is happen. If we did we'd have to talk to the RCMP guys and they'd want to know why we didn't go to the hospital and stuff. No use explain to them that Mad Etta be a good medicine doctor.

It is Sunday morning. We hear church bells ring off in the distance and I guess they is have some church service there after all.

When we get back to town most of the Indians is gone home already. It takes us a long time to get back and we bust two of the bikes carrying Mad Etta back to town. The town pretty quiet, some guys is carry the tables and chairs back into the bar, get it ready to open up again tomorrow.

The motorcycle guy is sure mad at us. He say he got the RCMP look for us cause we only supposed to have them bikes for three hours and we been gone for three days. I don't know why he get so excited, we always know we was going to bring them back.

It was late that afternoon that Annie Bottle is walk five miles up the old railway grade in her bare feet to give thanks for something. It sure hard to figure out what it might be.

The Inaugural Meeting

"Look at yourselves, Brothers!" yell Hobart Thunder. "Stop looking up here at me for a moment and turn and look at yourselves. Have you ever seen a more disgusting group? You look half-starved, half-dressed, half-alive!"

And on and on he go. Boy, he sure call us up one side and down another. We is, all us guys, down at the Blue Quills Hall at Hobbema Crossing, listen to this guy from the American Indian Movement give us a talk on Red Power.

All week there been posters up at the General Store and the Pool Hall at Hobbema showing this big red clenched fist hold on to a torch. The poster say Hobart Thunder, a founding member of the American Indian Movement, going to stop right here at Hobbema on his cross-country tour, speak to anybody who listen, silver collection, come at eight o'clock.

There is only about eight or so of us guys show up. Me, Frank and Charlie Fence-post, Eathen and Rufus Firstrider, Robert Coyote and maybe a couple of other guys sit on them

145

yellow wood chairs out on the basketball court in front of the stage while Hobart Thunder stand up there and talk like maybe he got a thousand or two people listen to him.

"You can't get no lower than you are now, Brothers! You are degraded, deprived, despised, trampled under the feet of Government bureaucracy. You are nothing!"

"Silas, you sure this here guy ain't white?" Frank say to me. "I sure never expect to hear an Indian talk to other Indians that way."

Hobart Thunder sure ain't white. In fact he don't look much different than us. He got long hair with a headband and a feather stick up behind him, a denim jacket, brown pants that too big for him and running shoes. He is old though, maybe 25.

What I wish though is that he would talk to us in his own voice. He keep read off little cards that he take out of the pocket of his jean jacket, like maybe without them he is going to forget some of the bad names he is call us.

"There is only one way for you to go and that is up! It is the job of myself and my brothers in the American Indian Movement to help you up from bondage, up from oppression, up from slavery!"

He pause there and I guess he expect us to clap our hands for him or something.

Everybody is sit silent. Hobart is look kind of worried for a minute, then he take a new card from his pocket and start up again.

There is two white guys is sit by themselves at the back of the hall. They got short hair, big muscles, clean jeans and denim jackets, and sport shirts that done right up to the collar. They might as well have on their bright red uniform and ride their horses.

"I was at Wounded Knee," Hobart say. "I saw my Red Brothers fight and die there on the Oglala Reservation during the seige. I saw the courage, the sacrifice, the bravery. Would you do the same for your reserve? Would you fight and die for," and here he stop and look on his card for help, "the Ermineskin Reserve and your town of Hobbema?"

Poor Hobart Thunder, he is make the mistake everybody else is. He think that just because Indians live here that Hobbema is an Indian name. People ask us all the time what Hobbema mean in Indian. Frank, he tell them it mean land of blue lakes, tall trees, running waters, with lots of buffalo that last as long as the grass shall grow. Only he tell it different to everyone who is ask. Hobbema was named by the white guys who built the Canadian Pacific Railway, it is the name of a Dutch guy who paint pictures a real long time ago.

"We been mostly peaceful, trusting and loyal for all these many years and look what that got us," Hobart go on. "We is the bottom men on the white man's totem pole. We got to fight! We got to burn! We got to destroy! Are you with me, Brothers?" And he give us the big Red Power salute, and bow a little, wait for us to clap our hands again. One or two of the guys do a little bit. Sound like somebody slap a couple of flies.

Hobart Thunder come down off the stage and sit with us. He have us put our chairs in a circle and we whisper a lot. He explain that the guys at the back of the hall is Feds that been sent to harass and disrupt his meetings. They is with the CIA and is follow him around all the time, only reason they don't do nothing tonight is that there is so few of us here.

Then he pull us in real close and whisper some more, but he is even whispering off the cards in his pocket.

"If you men believe in freedom for yourselves and your people, I want you should form the Ermineskin Warrior Society, right here and now. You may be a small group but with the guidance of the American Indian Movement you can make your presence felt all across your state – province – and maybe all across the country."

That name, Ermineskin Warrior Society, sure sound okay. It kind of sound exciting, and I can see myself lead a war party out to attack something, and I guess the other guys can too, cause we don't say nothing for a minute or so.

"Okay," say Hobart Thunder, and he pull

out a paper got a bunch of blanks for him to fill in. He sure have trouble get the right words in the right place, but finally he read off, "The inaugural meeting of the Hobbema Chapter of the Ermineskin Warrior Society come to order."

Then he get out some more notes and explain how we gonna make bombs with dynamite, blow up trains, even airplanes, and sometimes public buildings like this here hall we is in.

"How we gonna get money to build these bombs and stuff?" Rufus Firstrider ask.

"We could rob the stage," say Frank.

But Hobart got bigger ideas than that. We supposed to steal all the dynamite and stuff, he tell us. Then we is to rob banks and credit unions, and kidnap senators and other important guys, so we can collect lots of money to build more bombs.

Maybe it is just the way he tell his story, like he not quite believe it himself, that it don't sound like so good an idea to us. I look over at Eathen Firstrider and he screw up his nose. If Eathen don't like it that mean the rest of us don't either. But we don't want to hurt the feelings of Hobart Thunder, cause he seem like a nice man, and he sure come one long way to talk with us. So we try to look like we agree with what he tell us; we figure he go away and we never hear of him again.

"Now that the Ermineskin Warrior Society is organized, I want you should do something tonight," he say. "It be small, but it be," and he have to look at them cards in his pocket again, "a symbolic gesture. See them Feds sit back there? Well, their car is out front. I want volunteers to go out there and wreck the car!"

Frank put up his hand and take mine with it.

"Brother Ermineskin and Brother Fencepost have volunteered. The rest of you get closer to me and we keep on with our secret meeting so the Feds keep watching us. You guys pretend you going home."

Frank and me walk out of the hall. We stretch as we go past the Feds. "Boy, we is tired. We is going right home to bed," we say, but the Feds don't even look at us.

There is only three cars outside the hall. All of us guys came down in Eathen Firstrider's car, one that used to at one time belong to my brother-in-law, only he sort of left it on the reserve once when he come to visit. There is a beat-up 1969 Chevy with South Dakota plates and the back seat full of Red Power posters, and there is a new, silver, Ford LTD, look like it just drove out of a magazine. Them Feds sure must be rich guys.

We just stand look at it for a while. I don't mind if we steal it, cause boy, I sure would like to take Sadie One-wound, my girlfriend, for a ride in it, and maybe if I smart like Eathen, I get to keep it. I just don't like the idea of bust it up though, and Frank even though he act real brave, he don't much either.

I sort of kick a little dirt on the door.

"We got to remember it belong to them Feds," Frank say.

"I wish they'd tried to ... harass ... us so we could be really mad with them," I say. "Frank, maybe you pretend that the car belong to that RCMP guy who broke your nose in the back of the police car that time."

"I got even with him, Silas. I bled on his uniform good."

We have a little laugh about that, but Frank figure what I say is an okay idea. He take out his big jacknife and after quite a few tries cut one tire enough for the air to get out.

"Now it your turn," he say to me. "Who do you hate, Silas?"

I have to think for a minute, then I remember this dude that cheated me out of $50 when I was in the United States once. I just stand back and kick the middle of the passenger door with my steel-toed work boot and pretend that it the face of that guy who cheated me.

Frank take a rock and tap on a tail-light until it break. I do the same with a headlight. Then I find the doors ain't even locked. There is a bucket lay by the side of the hall.

"How about we wash this here car for the Feds?" I say.

Frank he get the idea and run down the hill to the slough and come back with a pail full half of mud and half of water. He step up and slop it right across the front seat.

"We got to wash the back too, hey?" I am starting to feel real good as I run down to the slough. Frank gets the rest of the tires flat by the time I come back with mostly mud in my bucket and toss it in the back seat.

We throw some rocks at the windows and windshield, they chip a little but they pretty hard to break. Our steel-toed boots sure dent in the sides good though, and we bust up every light on the car easy. Then Frank put up the hood and we pull out anything that come loose. Then we close up the hood and dance real hard on it until it cave in. We figure we fill up the gas tank with water but it got a lock on it so we kick off the tail-pipe instead. Then we put it in neutral, rock it some to get it started down the hill. It roll right into the slough, go schlo-o-o-o-mp, and sink about halfway out of sight.

It sure funny that to do something like that makes us feel so good. I think I can imagine what it be like to blow up a building.

We is sure a couple of proud guys when we go back to that meeting.

"Brother Hobart," we say, "we is strike the first blow for Red Power in Alberta," and he slap our backs and say maybe there is hope for us guys yet.

Brother Hobart sure change his tune when we all get outside.

"What did you guys do to my car," he yell.

"Ain't that your car?" we say, point at the 69 Chevy.

"That belongs to the Feds. The American Indian Movement is rent me a new car in Calgary to make my tour.

"We is sure sorry, Brother Hobart," we say.

He look like he just been hit in the stomach with a big red fist off one of his posters.

"Hey, Hobart," say one of the Feds. "You want a ride into town with us? We got a room right next to yours at the Alice Hotel."

"I guess that be okay," say Hobart.

"Come on," say the other CIA guy, "if we hurry up we can get there before the bar closes. We'll buy you a drink."

"I guess that be okay too," say Hobart.

"I hope you realize that's the second time that's happened on this tour. You got to remember to tell them which car is ours," say the first CIA guy. "That's why we drive the junker."

"We is sure sorry, Brother Hobart," we say again. Then we is all raise our fists in the Red Power salute as Hobart Thunder get in the back seat of the 69 Chevy.

Lark Song

If we'd been smart we never would have let Joseph go off by himself that Saturday in Wetaskiwin. But we did, and there sure been a lot of trouble for everybody ever since. My brother, Joseph Ermineskin, be older than me. He is 22 already, but when he just a baby he catch the scarlet fever and his mind it never grow up like his body do.

Joseph ain't crazy. He just got a tiny kid's mind in a big man's body. He is close to six feet tall and broad across the shoulder. His face is round and the colour of varnished wood. He be gentle and never hurt nobody in his whole life.

Unless you look right in his eyes he don't look no different than the rest of us guys. We let his hair grow long, and we got him a denim outfit, and once when I worked at a mine for the summer, I bought him a pair of cowboy boots. But Joseph he smile too often and too long at a time. I guess it because his mind ain't full of worries like everybody else.

Joseph ain't no more trouble to look after

154

than any other little kid and he is even good at a couple of things. He can hear a song on the radio and then play it back on my old guitar just like he heard it. He forget it pretty quick though, and can usually only do it one time.

And he can sound like birds. He caws like the crows so good that they come to see where the crow is that's talking to them. He talk like a magpie too, but best of all he sound like a meadowlark. Meadowlarks make the prettiest sound of any bird I ever heard, when they sing it sound like sweet water come bubble up out of a spring.

Sometime when we sit around the cabin at night and everyone is sad, Joseph he make that lark song for us and soon everyone is feel some better because it so pretty.

It is funny that he can do that sound so good, cause when he talk he sound like the wind-up record player when it not cranked up good enough. His voice is all slow and funny and he have to stop a long time between words.

One time, Papa, when he still lived here with us, is take Joseph with him to Wetaskiwin. Papa he get drunk and don't come home for a week or so, but the very next day, Joseph he is show up. He is hungry and tired from walk all those miles down the highway, but he find his way home real good. He is smile clear around to the back of his neck when he see us, and he don't ask about go to town with anybody for a long time after that.

Still I can tell he feel bad when me and my friend Frank Fence-post and all the guys go into town in Louis Coyote's pickup truck and leave him at home. That was why we take him one Saturday afternoon with us. We put him in the park to play while we go look in the stores and maybe stop for a beer or two. Joseph sure like the swings, and being strong and tall he can sure swing up high. What we should of told him though, and didn't, was for sure not to play with none of them white kids.

White people don't like nobody else to touch their kids, especially Indians. Here on the reserve it's kind of like one family, the kids run free when they is little and nobody minds if somebody else hugs your little boy or girl.

Joseph he like little kids and they like him back. Big people don't always have time, or maybe they don't want to, love their kids as much as they should. Joseph is pick up the kids when they fall down, or maybe when they is just lonesome. He don't say nothing to them, just pet their heads like maybe they was little kittens, hold them close and make them feel warm. Sometimes he make his bird sounds for them, and they forget whey they feel bad, hug his neck, and feel good that someone likes them.

People say that was what happen in the park in Wetaskiwin that day. A little white girl is fall

156

off the slide and hurt herself. When Joseph see her crying he is just pick her up like he would an Indian kid. Only them kids all been told, don't mess around with strangers, and somebody runs for some mothers.

We come back to get Joseph about the same time that little girl's mother come to get her. If you ever seen a lady partridge fly around on the ground pretend she got a broken wing so her enemy go after her and leave her young ones alone, that is how that white lady is act.

Joseph is just stand in the sandbox hold that little girl in his arms, and she is not even crying anymore until she hear her mother scream and dance up and down. I sure afraid for what might have happen to Joseph if we don't come when we did.

I unwrap his arms from the little girl and hand her back to the lady, who is cry some and yell a lot of bad things at us and say somebody already called the RCMP.

The RCMP guys come roll up in their car with the lights flash and I sure wish we was all someplace else. While everyone try to yell louder than everyone else, Joseph he sit down and play some in the sand and every once in a while he is make his meadowlark call.

I try to explain to them RCMP guys that Joseph he is about as harmless as that meadowlark he is sounding like. Meadowlarks ain't very pretty or good for much but make beautiful sounds, but they sure don't hurt nobody either, I tell them.

Lots of people is standing around watching and I think they figure something real bad has happened. There is a real big white lady with a square face is carry a shotgun.

We promise the RCMP guys and anybody else that will listen that for sure we never gonna bring Joseph to town no more. We keep him on the reserve forever and then some, we tell them.

For once it look like maybe the RCMP is gonna believe us Indians. They say they can't see no reason to lay any charges, cause all it look like Joseph done was to pick up a kid that fall down. The white girl's mother is yell loud on everybody, say if the RCMP ain't gonna do nothing she'll go to somebody who will. And that lady with the square face wave her shotgun and say she would sure like to shoot herself a few wagon-burners.

After we all go to the police station for a while the RCMP guys let us take Joseph home, but it is only a couple of days until some Government people is come nose around our place a lot. They is kind of like the coyotes come pick at the garbage, we hardly ever see them but we still know they is there.

Two little women in brown suits come to our cabin, say wouldn't we think Joseph be happier in a home someplace where there are lots of other retarded guys.

Ma, like she always do, pretend she don't understand English, and just sit and look at them with a stone face. But she sure is worried.

Next time they come back, they ain't nearly so nice. They say either we put Joseph in the place for crazy people at Ponoka, or they get a judge to tell us we have to.

The next week, me and my girlfriend Sadie One-wound, hitch-hike the twelve miles to Ponoka to have a look at the crazy place. I know all my life that the place is there but there is something about a place like that that scares us a lot. It makes us too shy to go up to the gate and ask to look around. Instead we just walk around outside for a while. It got big high wire fences but inside there is lots of grass and beds of pretty flowers, and the people who walk around inside don't look as though they trying to run away or nothing.

The Government peoples keep sending Ma big fat letters with red writing on them. One say that Ma and Joseph got to appear at something called a committal hearing at the court room in Wetaskiwin. We figure that if we go there they gonna take Joseph away from us for sure.

I go down to the pay phone at Hobbema Crossing and phone all the way to Calgary to the office of Mr. William Wuttunee, the Indian lawyer, but he is away on holiday, and no, I say, I don't want nobody to call me or nothing.

We don't go to that committal hearing

cause Ma, she say that we just pretend that nothing is happening, and if we do that long enough the white people stop bothering us.

A couple of weeks later we get another big bunch of papers with red seals all over them, delivered by the RCMP guys personal. Them papers say they gonna come and get Joseph on a certain date. We figure it out on the calendar from the Texaco Service Station, and we decide that when they come they ain't gonna find no Joseph. We just put him to live with someone back in the bush a few miles and move him around whenever we have to.

One good thing about white people is that they usually give up easy. The RCMP is always nose around for Sam Standing-at-the-door's still, or maybe have a warrant for arrest somebody for steal car parts or something, but we tear up the culvert in the road from Hobbema to our cabins, and them guys sure hate to walk much, so they just go away after they yell at the closest Indians for a while. We figure the Government people like to walk even less than the RCMP so it be pretty easy to fool them.

I don't know if they came a day early or if maybe we forget a day someplace, but their cars is already across the culvert and halfway up the hill before we see them. And the guy from the crazy place in Ponoka, who wears a white jacket, look like he be a cook in a café, say he is a Métis, and he even talk Cree to us, which is real bad, cause then we can't pretend we don't understand, especially if we sharpen a knife or play with a gun while we talk about them some in our language.

This Métis guy tell us, look, they ain't gonna hurt Joseph down there at the mental hospital, and it only be twelve miles away so we can come visit him anytime. He gonna be warm and clean and have lots of food and he get to make friends with other guys like him and maybe even learn to make things with his hands and stuff.

It don't sound so bad after all, if it true what he says. All we had time to do was hide Joseph under the big bed in the cabin, and he been making bird songs all the time he is under there. Ma, she finally call him to come out, and he poke his head and smile on everybody.

We pack up his clothes in a cardboard box. He sure ain't got much to take with him. Frank Fence-post ask them guys if they got electric light down at the crazy place, and they tell him the hospital is fully equipped. Frank he goes and gets his fancy-shaped electric guitar that he bought at a pawnshop in Calgary. He tell the guys from the hospital they should show Joseph how to plug the guitar into the wall. Then he shove the guitar into Joseph's arms.

The kids is all come out from the cabins and stand around look shy at the ground while I talk to Joseph, like I would my littlest sister, explain he should be good, and how these guys is his friends and all. Joseph he pet the guitar like it alive and smile for everybody and touch his fingers on the shiny paint of the car from Ponoka.

Once they is gone we sure ain't got much to say to each other. Me and Frank talk a little about how we go visit Joseph on Saturday, sneak him away and hide him out on the reserve. But it different when they got him than when we got him, and I don't think that idea ever gonna come to much.

I don't sleep so good that night. I am up early. The sky is clear and the sun is just come up. There is frost on the brown grasses and the slough at the foot of the hill is frozen thin as if window glass had been laid across it. Brown bulrushes tipped with frost, stand, some straight, some at angles, like spears been stuck in the ground. Outside the cabin door our dogs lie curled like horse collars in their dirt nests. They half open their yellow eyes, look at me then go to sleep again. The air is thin and clear and pine smoke from another cabin is rise straight up like ink lines on paper. From the woodpile I carry up an armful of split pine. The wood is cold on my arm and I tuck the last piece under my chin.

Then there is like an explosion from down the hill and across the slough someplace. Like a gun shot, only beautiful. The crows rise up like they been tossed out of the spruce trees.

At first I want to laugh it sound so funny, the voice of a summer bird on a frosty morning. Then it come again, that sweet, bubbly, blue-sky-coloured lark song. I do laugh then, but for happy, and I toss the wood on the ground and run for the meadow.

Feathers

It was about three months before the big important Council of Indian Tribes meeting in Calgary that Mrs. Chief Tom Crow-eye decide to become a chicken dancer, and that is about the last thing that her husband is want her to do.

Chief Tom Crow-eye is what militant Indians call an apple. He is red on the outside but white on the inside. Lucky for him there ain't many militant Indians around the Ermineskin Reserve, so he probably be our chief for quite a long time. There is talk about Chief Tom gonna run for the Conservative Party in the next election here in Alberta. And, boy, if you don't think that make him feel more important than he already is, you better think again. He tell everybody who get in his way that he been reading books on political science and study up on the constitution.

"You ever do any experiments in that there political science?" my friend Frank Fence-post ask him one time, "Like make up stuff to smell like rotten eggs, the way we do sometimes down to the Technical School."

"No," Chief Tom say to Frank, and look down on him like maybe he a pile of cow chips. Us guys talk about some time we gonna put Frank Fence-post up for chief. We say if we gonna have a chief don't do nothing for us, we should elect one that be really good at it.

Chief Tom is pretty young as Indian chiefs go, only about 40, and his wife, Mary, be five years or so younger. He is a pretty handsome guy, even though he is awful short and a little bow-legged. Used to be that the tribal war bonnet, that some say belonged to Poundmaker, drag on the ground behind him when he wear it. They say he took it to a tailor shop in Edmonton and got it shortened. Frank Fence-post make jokes on him when he ain't around, say if Chief Tom was ever to lead us into battle, he be able to ride on a big dog instead of a war pony. Sometimes when he is around, somebody say, "Bow-wow, bow-wow," and everybody is bust up laughing, and Chief Tom is always wonder why.

Even before I know for sure, I suspected that it be because of Samantha Yellowknees that Mrs. Chief Tom decide to become a chicken dancer. Mrs. Chief Tom Crow-eye is not what most people would say is a pretty woman. She is stocky built, no real fat, but she run pretty straight up and down. She got heavy legs and walk flat-footed like a man. She have a wide, flat face, small eyes and a big wide mouth with spaces between her teeth. She is jolly though and she got a fine laugh, and nobody ever mistake her smile for anything else.

Samantha Yellowknees come from Ontario and been to the University someplace. She is about 25, live in Wetaskiwin and work on some Government project that is supposed to help Indians some way. Samantha be pretty in a school teacher kind of way, wears her hair pulled back, got glasses with diamonds in the rims, and wears Indian clothes that she bought in a department store, all covered in beads and elk teeth and feathers made from plastic.

Right from the start Chief Tom sure take a big interest in Samantha's project and they sure have lots of business to talk about. She come out to the reserve, picks him up in her shiny little Government car with racing stripes and wheel covers. They talk their business mainly at the cocktail lounge of the Travelodge Hotel and I think sometimes at her apartment over on 51st Avenue in Wetaskiwin. I never been in the Travelodge cocktail lounge, but me and Frank peeked in the door one night and seen how dark it was and how the furniture is covered in dark red leather. It don't look like a place to laugh a lot and I hear they charge a dollar for a bottle of beer.

Before he met up with Samantha, Chief Tom used to wear work pants and a blue windbreaker. Then he got him a suit from the Eaton's Catalogue, be baggy around his bottom and have big cuffs. Now he wears woolly jackets, a white shirt and ties that Samantha buys for him from Robinson's Stores.

It ain't too long before the chief be taking Samantha along on his trips to Edmonton and Calgary. It make me feel some sorry for the chief's wife. Nothing is ever a secret very long around the reserve and Mrs. Chief Tom must know all about what going on, but I guess all she can do is pretend that it don't happen.

Us guys go around sometimes, watch Mrs. Chief Tom practise her chicken dance. She get Rufus Firstrider to play the drum for her and she dance around in the yard in front of their house. Now the chicken dance be a really fast one and usually only done by really good dancers. It kind of sad but there don't be no way that anybody could say that Mrs. Chief Tom be a good dancer. Her legs is too heavy and her body too fat, and she have a hard time squat down a lot and shake her backside like a chicken dancer supposed to do.

None of us got the bad heart to tell her she ain't no good, cause she be really excited about it and say she figure she be able to help out Chief Tom to get him elected and stuff, if she do her dance at meetings where he gonna speak. Everybody I know is like Mrs. Chief Tom and I bet a lot of people, like me for one, is vote on him for chief mainly because of his wife be such a nice lady. When we was little, Mary Crow-eye used to let us guys hang around her place. She used to laugh a lot, tell us stories, and give us tea that was mostly milk with lots of brown sugar in it.

Pretty soon, everybody around the reserve know about Mrs. Crow-eye be a dancer. We sure know that Chief Tom ain't gonna like it, cause a chicken dance be about as Indian as you can get and Chief Tom he try to get whiter every day. I bet they sure have some good arguments about that at the Crow-eye house. If there be one thing that Chief Tom like to do it is repeat himself, so I bet even if he can only think of one or two reasons for his wife not to dance he make it seem like 50. Neighbours say they can hear Chief Tom yell for about half a mile, but I guess it don't do no good, cause every day Rufus is play the drum and Mrs. Chief Tom is dance in the yard.

"I'm gonna dance at the Council of Indian Tribes meeting when we go to Calgary," she tell everybody.

"You ain't gonna be just a scalp on Chief Tom's belt, are you?" I say to her, but guess she too busy dancing to listen to the radio, so she don't get the joke.

One night, me, Frank, Rufus, and few other guys are just on our way into the Alice Hotel beer parlour in Wetaskiwin when we meet up with Chief Tom coming out of the dining room. He got Mr. J. William Oberholtzer, Mayor of Wetaskiwin and President of the Conservative Party with him.

"Hey, young fellows," he says to us, "I sure hate to see you young people spending your time in bars."

"It be some better than behind them," says Frank.

"I suppose it is," say Chief Tom, and he make a polite little laugh. All last winter Chief Tom went one night a week into Edmonton to take a course in public speaking. I guess he did pretty good at it, cause now he can talk for a long time about just about anything and sound as if he know all about it even if he don't.

"This is an example of one of the things we were discussing over dinner, Mr. Mayor. What this community needs badly is more recreational facilities for our young people so that they don't have to spend their time in taverns...." Mr. J. William Oberholtzer wrinkle up his face and step back so he sure none of us don't touch him.

"How about if you come in buy us all a round, Chief Tom?" say Frank.

"Young fellow, I don't think you understood what I was just saying. Under no circumstances do I want to contribute to the degradation of my people." He kind of puff up his chest when he say this and talk louder than he need to.

"I think he say no," Rufus whispers pretty loud.

"I want you young fellows to consider something for a moment. How many important people do you meet in beer parlours? How many doctors or lawyers do you meet in there?"

"Or Indian chiefs," we say and jump up and down some.

"Think about it," Chief Tom say with a real solemn face. "You don't see the Mayor or other important people drinking in beer parlours. You have to associate with people of value if you ever want to amount to anything."

"I got reservations about that," say Rufus. Chief Tom don't get the joke and he figures he gonna get in a political argument until he sees us all laugh so much.

"Yeah, well if you won't come in why don't you just loan us a couple of bucks and we'll think good thoughts about you while we is drinking?" says Frank.

"As you can see, Mr. Mayor," Chief Tom says, like maybe he is talking on television, "there is still a great deal to be accomplished. However, I'm sure that if we persevere...."

"Bow-wow, bow-wow," says Frank, and everybody is break up with laughter. A couple of us even roll on the sidewalk as Chief Tom and the Mayor walk away shake their heads about us.

If she'd wanted to, Mrs. Chief Tom could probably of borrowed a chicken dancer costume from Eli Longlegs or one of the other guys who do the chicken dance at ceremonies or special occasions. But she decide to make her own. The chicken dance be named not for the barnyard chicken but for the prairie chicken who is fan out his tail and make a lot of thumping sounds like soldiers marching.

Me and Frank and Rufus gather up feathers for her to use. We get most of them by shoot a couple of prairie chicken with Rufus' .22, but what look best is the eagle and hawk feathers that we find back in the hills. Mrs. Chief Tom gets bark and roots and leaves and makes up dyes just like our medicine lady, Mad Etta do. The dyes you make yourself come out the purest colours of red, blue and green that I ever seen.

"Mad Etta show me how to make these dyes when I was just a girl. I be pretty lazy about a lot of things but at least I don't buy Nabob Food Colouring for put on my face and my feathers."

One day when we having tea alone at her place, she say to me, "I'm gonna make Tom like me again. You wait and see." She look pretty sad when she say this and her lips be like a big red rubber band stretched across her face.

I wait and see, but I feel some sad for Mrs. Chief Tom because she be about the only one who don't see that she be worth ten Chief Toms and even more Samanthas. But I don't know how you tell somebody something like that so I don't say nothing.

Lots of important people be at the Council of Indian Tribes meeting in Calgary. It be kind of mixed up with the Alberta election or something and there be about as many white people there as Indians. Only difference be that the meeting be held outdoors, in the big park near the zoo. If it been a white man meeting it be held at the Auditorium or the Corral, guess after a while Indians believe what they told about themselves. They got big log tables set up for everybody to eat at. The really important people are at the head table on the platform and they all going to make speeches after we eat. There is red, white and blue banners all over and the Premier himself is sit right up on the stage and smile just like poster of himself that is behind him. Mrs. Premier Lougheed is right there beside him, in a pretty red dress and her hair done up fancy. There is Mr. Maurice Tailfeathers, Chief of the Bloods, all dressed up in his war bonnet and buckskins, and his lady, in a white deerskin dress.

On the other side of the Premier is Chief Tom, he got on a suit of that Conservative blue colour, kind of glow every time the sun shine on it. He been to the beauty parlour for men and got his hair cut just like Premier Lougheed. He even got grey sprayed into the sides which I bet was Samantha Yellowknees' idea. The chair next to him be empty.

Chief Tom keep getting up and sitting down like he got an itch or something. He walks to the back of the stage and sees me and Frank hanging around.

"Have you young fellows seen my wife?" he says to us.

"No," we tell him, "but we go look for her if you like."

"The speeches are going to start soon. Everybody will wonder about it if she's not here."

We seen Mrs. Chief Tom around a half-hour or so before and she sure be a pretty bad sight. That afternoon Chief Tom is send her downtown to the beauty parlour with a note tell them to make her real pretty, and he had Samantha buy her some fancy clothes to sit up on the platform with. She had on a bright green dress made out of a kind of crêpe-papery stuff, and her hair was coiled up on top of her head look like a wasp's nest. Mrs. Chief Tom ain't meant to look like no white lady, that hairdo made her forehead seem most a foot high, and she had on a pair of bright red platform shoes that made her as tall as Samantha Yellowknees. Somebody put rouge on her cheeks which be pretty high to start with, and she got on green earrings look like slices of cucumber. I sure don't think Samantha tried very hard when she picked out them clothes for Mrs. Crow-eye. Samantha got on a dress the colour of lemon pie, with a white collar make her look cool even though everybody else is sweat. She got her hair tied back in a bun, and carry around a clipboard with a lot of writing on it, and she remind Chief Tom of things all the time.

Frank and me start off to look for the Chief's wife when all of a sudden we hear Rufus start to beat the drum and everybody is look to where he sit cross-legged in front of the stage, his cowboy hat so far down over his eyes that I wonder how he can see the drum at all. Then, out from under the stage, come Mrs. Chief Tom. She be all dressed up in her chicken-dancer costume, and her face and arms be dyed with war paint the same colour as her feathers. She must of combed all that glue-stuff out of her hair cause she got a buffalo-horn headdress on. Everyone sure surprised cause there not supposed to be no entertainment until late in the evening. Everybody just sit around and watch her dance, everybody that is except Chief Tom. First he walk up and down behind the head table, then he go down the back steps and head off a ways so he don't have to look at her. It easy to tell he be plenty upset. Samantha be right there beside him and as they walk she be write a whole lot on her clipboard.

Chief Tom ain't the only one who be embar-

174

rassed. It pretty hard for us other Indians too, cause no matter how hard Mrs. Chief Tom try, she be one awful dancer.

"Maybe we call that a wounded buffalo dance," say Frank Fence-post.

But the joke be on us. When she is finish up, the Indian people don't do nothing, or clap just a little to be polite, but the white people, and there be a whole lot of them there, including guys from the newspaper and television take pictures, clap like they just seen the Calgary Stampeders make a touchdown. Mrs. Chief Tom have to bow about three times before she go back under the stage.

We listen to them white people talk and they sure figure she was something special. What we forget I guess is that white people be so dumb about Indian things. They figure that somebody who put on feathers and dance has got to be good.

A few minutes later Chief Tom comes back. It look to me like he take a big breath at the top of the hill, leave Samantha stand there, and come march right down like he going to a battle. He come in and start right away to apologize for what his wife done. People sure look at him funny but Chief Tom never been one to understand how people is feeling. When Chief Tom start to talk it be pretty hard to shut him up cause I think one of the things he like to hear best is his own voice. He get quite a group around him and the last part of his speech be something like this.

"When I first started out I used to work for the railroad, cutting brush along the right of way. I was a labourer in those days. When Mary married me she married a labourer. But that was a long time ago, and I've been pretty lucky, got myself a better job, got to be chief, but unfortunately Mary is still a labourer's wife. She hasn't moved along with me."

While he been talking Mrs. Chief Tom is come out from under the stage. She changed her clothes and got on a green mackinaw jacket over a housedress, her face and arms still be coloured with war paint and she hold her chicken dancer costume in her arms. Chief Tom say a whole lot of other things to try and not make himself look bad, but what Mary Crow-eye hear was just that last part.

Samantha has come back and is trying to get through the crowd to Chief Tom. She is kind of chopping her way through with her clipboard. People like Samantha can smell bad situations.

Chief Tom is not even notice that his wife is there or that people is want to shake her hand for do such a good dance. A radio guy is there, look like he got a parachute on his back and keep poke a microphone into Mrs. Chief Tom's face, but I guess all she be able to hear is the speech the chief is make about her, cause she turn and push her way through the crowd. On the way she meet up with Samantha Yellow-knees and she shove into her arms her chicken dance costume, so hard that it knock Samantha's clipboard right out of her hands. Some of the eagle feathers we gathered puff up in the air and drift for a minute before they fall back into the crowd.

Premier Lougheed is come down off the platform and right over to Chief Tom. Before the chief can start to apologize, the Premier tell him how much he like the dance and say he figure with the combination of the chief's personality and Mrs. Chief's dancing, they going to make one fine candidate for the next election. Then he tell Chief Tom that in a few minutes he going to announce to the crowd that the chief got his support for the Conservative nomination for Wetaskiwin.

It take Chief Tom a minute or two to catch on that everything be okay after all, then he sure quick to agree with what the Premier say. The Premier go back to the platform and the chief start to look around for his wife. But I guess I is about the only one who can see her. She still be walking across the park and be just a black dot up high on one of the green hills.

Between

The trouble was that Rider Stonechild want Mad Etta to do something that she don't really want to. I was there at Mad Etta's cabin when he come to see her. Etta was sitting on her tree-trunk chair having a smoke and a beer. Rider he sure seem to be upset cause he hardly even say hello to me.

"Etta I got to talk to you. You got to do something for me."

Then he look real hard at me. His look say, "Silas, you better go home." I finish my beer in one swallow and stand up to go. I don't want no trouble with Rider Stonechild. He's about 45, wide at the shoulders and about six feet tall. He got shiny black hair that he comb up to a peak at the front, the sides are long, combed backward, and got a lot of silver in them. That silver make him pretty handsome Indian. He got on a blue check mackinaw shirt that his arms fill right up, light brown pants and work boots that lace up past his ankles. Rider he got a good job with the UGG Elevator at Wetaskiwin.

"It be okay for Silas to stay," Mad Etta say.

"This here is private personal stuff I want to talk about."

"It still be okay. Silas be kind of my assistant."

I don't know nothing about this before except that Mad Etta been pretty nice to me lately. I figure maybe pretty soon she was gonna ask me to drive her up to Edmonton or something.

"Personal stuff," Rider say again, and look arrows at me. I move my chair back in the corner where I almost hid in the shadows. Etta and him talk and argue for most an hour. He wants her to make a potion for him to give somebody. He get pretty ugly. He don't say right out that he gonna hurt her if she don't but it pretty easy to get that idea from the way he say things. Etta finally say she'll think on it. Then she hold up her hand like an old-time Indian to show him that there be no more talk about it right then. Rider he go away grumbling.

What it amount to be that Rider Stonechild got white man troubles and he want to use Indian ways to get out of them. He's had that good job with the UGG quite a few years. He don't drink much so he got things pretty good. He live with his wife, Mary-Therese, and a few kids in a nice home on the reserve. The house is painted and they got a car that runs. Then not too long ago Rider, he got himself a girlfriend.

Nothing that goes on around the reserve is a secret very long and soon everybody is know that Rider be out to the beer parlour a lot with Darlene Roche who work at the Gulf Service Station Coffee Shop across from the elevators. She only be about twenty or so, maybe be Métis, or maybe just a dark white girl. She come from Manitoba and live in a basement room about a block from the Alice Hotel.

Darlene she got a round face with red cheeks and big wide spaces between all her teeth, and she laugh loud at everything anybody say to her. She got real full lips and she wear white lipstick the same colour as her coffee-shop uniform. She sure is different from Rider's wife who been a convent girl. Guess maybe that is why he like Darlene so much, cause she be different.

"How come you take guff from a guy like Rider?" I ask as soon as he's gone. Usually some guy get out of line with Etta she just run him off quick. I seen her one time throw Charlie Fence-post right through the screen door of her cabin, and he was only making fun on her, not ordering her to do something for him.

"Silas, you got to learn to look inside people. You got to size them up like they was a stack of beer glasses. You listen and you look real close until you see which one got the fly in it. Then you figure how to get the fly out without knocking down the whole stack. That what doctoring be all about."

"Why do I gotta learn that? You be the medicine lady."

"Cause I'd like maybe for you to be my assistant. I got to pick somebody, and learn them the things I know."

"Maybe I don't want to be your assistant."

"Silas, you be about the only one of the young people who don't make fun of what I do. You read me all them funny stories you write for Mr. Nichols, and it make me kind of proud that you an Ermineskin Indian, even if I don't think you should tell personal stuff about us in white man's papers."

Mr. Nichols down to the Technical School in Wetaskiwin, read my stories and gets the school secretary to type them up. He corrects my spellings and puts in those commas and stuff, but he say he leave the syntax like it is. He explain syntax to me once but I didn't understand much. I just glad Mr. Nichols like it enough to leave it alone.

"If I was your assistant I'd of run Rider Stonechild out of here when he started calling you names."

"You know I was down to the white-man hospital one time," Mad Etta say. "They cut something out of my belly, lucky they be able to find it for all the fat," she say, and laugh and laugh, blowing clouds of smoke over top of the coal-oil lamp.

"But first they take pictures of my insides with a machine. I ain't got no machine. All I got is my eyes. If you'd been looking at Rider Stonechild instead of peeling the paper off your beer bottle you'd of seen it's the top glass that got the fly in it. And that be the toughest one to fix up. Rider kind of caught between the old and new."

"He got himself a girlfriend and a wife that don't like him to have no girlfriend. Those is white man's troubles. What's old or new about that?"

"Silas, when I was a girl, if a man be a good enough hunter to provide for two wives, he don't have to ask nobody he just go ahead and move that new wife into his lodge. Everybody is know their place in those days. The first wife still be number one woman, she don't lose no face by have that happen. The man he gain more respect for afford two wives and the wives be proud be the wives of a rich man."

"Things have changed," I say.

"The world's kind of a hard place for men like Rider Stonechild. Guys like Rider they was born into the old ways. His parents travelled around in the summer, lived in tipis, hunted, made their own clothes. Rider he had to change his ways right in the middle of his life. How you think you'd feel, Silas, if all of a sudden you had to go out and hunt your food, have a horse pulling a travois to carry your grub, and your hides for make a tent, and have no cans to open when you hungry?"

"I guess I'd be pretty lost."

"See Rider done pretty good for himself. He worked for the white man without his skin turning white like Chief Tom and some other guys we all know. But now that he got white man's troubles he want to use the old ways to cure them. The old ways die hard."

I never realize that there be so much to being a medicine man.

"I hate to get mixed up in love things, especially where somebody be sneak around. It hardly ever turn out good. That's why I argue with him so much. If I didn't feel some sorry for Rider, I wouldn't help him. But I sure don't want him even to guess that I be sorry for him."

"So what are you gonna do?"

"Much as I can I'm gonna help him."

"By doing what? He don't even know for sure what he want you to do. 'Make me some strong medicine, Etta,' he say. 'Look into the future and get me out from under my trouble.'"

"You and me will decide, Silas. That be your first job as my assistant. But it don't look to me like there be much to decide. If he wanted his girlfriend he be gone with her by now. My father used to say a wise thing to me, he claim it was said for the first time by Poundmaker. 'If you want something and you don't know how to get it then you don't want it bad enough.' Together we fix up some medicine make Darlene the girlfriend go away," and she hold up her hand to show me we don't talk no more about it right then. Somehow it don't seem to me that I have much to do with make that decision, but I guess if Mad Etta think I do, then it be okay.

While he was at Mad Etta's Rider Stonechild is yell a lot about how his wife she gonna sick some lawyer fellow on him, and I hear from my girlfriend, Sadie One-wound, who hang around with the ladies down to Blue Quills Hall in the afternoons, that what happens is when Mary-Therese start to give Rider trouble about him run around with Darlene, why he tell her to shut up, like he would an old-time Indian lady, or maybe he rearrange her face some.

Only trouble is Mary-Therese ain't no old-time Indian lady. She been to grade twelve at the convent school, belong to clubs at church, get magazines in her mail, and even belong to the Conservative Party, get people to vote on Premier Lougheed.

Mary-Therese instead of shut up, goes to a lawyer up in Edmonton. A white lawyer who go and tell her all about all the rights she got, but mostly about all the rights Rider don't have.

Next morning I get to help Mad Etta make up a medicine bag. All across one wall of her cabin she got shelves nailed up. And them shelves be lined with tobacco tins, maybe 40 or 50 of them, in yellow, blue, green and red. Each one got in it something different: flower seeds, roots, bark, porcupine quills, pig bristles and lots of things I don't know about that look scary and smell worse.

She put things from maybe a dozen cans into a saucepan and simmer it on the back of her wood stove for most of the day. It make the cabin smell like burning tires. Then toward evening she squeeze most of the water out of that stuff and pack what's left inside the hide of a chipmunk that she snared and skinned. Then she have me hang the medicine bag up high in a spruce tree back of her cabin.

"Tomorrow it be ready to do its work," she say to me, and crack us a couple of bottles of Lethbridge Pale Ale that been sit in a pail of water on her porch, their labels floating around like drowned mice.

Rider comes by that evening and I be surprised at the way Mad Etta handle him. No more listen and take insults.

"Tomorrow, I make medicine," she tell him in a serious voice. "Go to work like usual. Stay away from your women until evening. Now go away from me."

Etta turn her back on him then. From behind she look big as a buffalo. I guess it be the tone of her voice that make Rider Stonechild do like she wants. She just stay silent when he ask what it is she gonna do, and when he goes I pretty sure I hear him say thank you, real low, as he close the door.

Next morning, first thing, I cut down the medicine bag and give it to Mad Etta. Then I borrow Blind Louis Coyote's pickup truck to drive Mad Etta to Wetaskiwin. It be a big job get Etta in and out of the truck. She way too big for sit in the cab so she ride in the back. We go and get the door from One-wound's outhouse and use it for a ramp. Then I get my friends Frank Fence-post and Rufus Firstrider and one pull and two push her up into the truck. We first put her tree-trunk chair up there for her to sit on. On the way to town Frank and Rufus ride up front with me.

Mad Etta she dressed up some for the trip to town. She put some stripes of red and blue dye on her face, and down each sleeve of her five-flour-sack dress she is pin five squirrel tails. She got the medicine bag in one hand and in the other a calf skull filled with pebbles and wrapped in buckskin.

We drive up to Wetaskiwin and stop right in front of the Gulf Oil Service Station Coffee Shop, unload Mad Etta and she waddle inside. She only be gone a couple of minutes and she got some big fat smiles for us when she come out. While we is load her up again, Darlene Roche and some other people is stand in the window of the café and look funny at us. Darlene's face be about as white as her lipstick.

Before we go home we all go over to the Alice Hotel beer parlour and buy Mad Etta some beer. We is all pretty happy.

Back at Mad Etta's we is celebrate some more and I get to figuring that maybe it be a good idea if I be Mad Etta's assistant. But when I tell her that she say, "One thing you got to remember is that you can't ever tell your friends how you do nothing. It be one thing to have friends. It another be a medicine man. Never tell nobody any of your secrets, and even if something you do be easy as breathe in and out, pretend that it hard for you. Always act like you're right and like everything gonna be okay, even if you're scared as hell."

Just then Frank Fence-post come by to say he heard Darlene decided kind of quick that her health gonna be bad if she stay around Wetaskiwin. He say she quit her job right in the middle of her shift and catch the southbound bus, still wearing her uniform and carrying only a shopping bag.

We sure laugh some about that and give Frank a beer. It make Etta feel real proud that her medicine work so good. She say it be a good sign, maybe even mean that I should keep on to help her. She feel so good that after Frank leave she talk for most an hour about what it like to be a medicine man.

187

Then my girlfriend, Sadie One-wound, come running in. Sadie got some bad news and say maybe me and Etta should go someplace else for a while cause Rider Stonechild be over at Blind Louis' drinking moonshine and calling us out. Seems that nobody ever told Mary-Therese that Mad Etta was going to fix things up. Not that a convent girl like her would of believed. What she done is today she changed the lock on her house and while Rider was at work she take the car and have the lock changed on it too. And this afternoon her lawyer serve some papers on Rider at work tell him that Mary-Therese is want a divorce and that she gonna take most of his wages for support her, the kids, the house, the car and the lawyer.

After we hear that we ain't so happy anymore. Mad Etta say to me that I better get Sadie out of there and that she'll stay and talk to Rider if he comes. But before I get a chance to answer, Rider Stonechild comes bust through the door toting a big old .303 rifle and he got moonshine on his breath and a mean look in his eye.

"Everybody claim you can see into the future," he yell at Mad Etta. She just sit on her tree-trunk chair and stare at him. Sadie hugs my arm and I push her back so she stand behind my chair.

Rider got the gun pointed right up against Mad Etta's big flat nose. "Tell me what you see in the future now? You make big medicine alright. My wife's gonna take everything away from me and Darlene's left me. You tell me how you gonna keep from dying? Tell me!" Boy, his whole big body be tremble some when he say that.

"I always knew that I was going to die," Mad Etta say real quiet and slow. "But I never know when, until now. All I've known for a long time, a long time, is that I been going to die three days before you, Rider Stonechild."

I sure hope Rider ain't had too much moonshine to understand that. I see my hand shaking even though it hanging on to the edge of the table. Etta got her right eye closed, but she looking steady at Rider with her left one, staring right back up the barrel at his eye that look through the gun sight. In the shadows of the coal-oil light I bet Rider feel kind of like he looking down a gopher hole. I keep look at the lamp, the wick is burn high on one corner making black streaks all up one side of the chimney.

Longhouse

In the beginning, everybody is try to talk Poppy Twelvetrees out of going to the city. Especially Charlie Cardinal who is kind of figure he own her. She been Charlie's girl since she was about fourteen.

I guess it was Charlie she told first cause it is him who tell everybody else. He be really mad about her going to do a crazy thing like that. Charlie is 22, stocky as an oil drum, got big strong hands, and a bad scar from his hair to his eyebrow that he got when a horse pitched him into the fence at the Rimbey Rodeo. Charlie and Poppy been promised to each other, which mean that she ain't supposed to fool around with nobody else, and that Charlie going to marry her, when he get good and ready.

Poppy Twelvetrees be eighteen only a couple of weeks before she decide to go to the city. Poppy is one of those girls who move nice naturally. She be wide-shouldered and have big breasts, her hair is long and look like it never been combed even after she just finish combing it. Down at the Blue Quill Hall at the Saturday night dances all the white guys go after her, and Charlie been in more than one fight on account of that. She wears a skirt made up from a couple of pairs of old jeans, a bright green blouse and on the back of the skirt, with embroidery, she made some yellow flowers look like cowslips. Poppy be about the best dancer around. She move graceful and what is best about it is that she don't realize how good she is. To her, dancing just come natural. I sit sometimes on bench along the wall at the dance hall just to watch her when they play some rock music. I picture her dance naked, which I suppose ain't very nice of me, but that is just the way she make me feel.

Charlie yell at her a lot and tell her she ain't going to go to Edmonton, no way. They argue a lot when we are all down at the pool hall at Hobbema in the afternoons. But it just be two separate people giving speeches: Poppy say she going to go, Charlie say she ain't.

Some of us guys who been to the city try to talk to her, tell her how Indian girls sure get into a lot of trouble up there. Suzie Calf-robe went to Calgary a couple of years ago, and she be drink and fight and stuff and sell herself to the oil drillers for maybe five or ten dollars. I seen her there one time and though she be only about nineteen she look like 30, her cheeks be all puffy, she had a couple of her teeth knocked out, and she got blue tattoos on both her arms.

The arguments always end in a tie though, us saying one thing and Poppy the other. Charlie even offer to marry her right away. He say they'll go to Wetaskiwin get the licence, have the priest marry them maybe next week. He even say he take her down to Calgary for a couple of days' honeymoon. I bet a year or so ago Poppy Twelvetrees would have gone for that real quick, but not anymore.

"I'm gonna build us a cabin, Poppy," Charlie say to her. "This summer I make lots of money ride in the rodeos. We'll pick out furniture from a store in Wetaskiwin and ... "

"I've made up my mind, Charlie," she say, and go walk out of the pool hall all alone.

It was right after this that Mr. Ernest Paul come into the pool hall and Charlie Cardinal be so desperate that he ask him for advice. Mr. Ernest Paul be with the Indian Affairs Department, don't do much of any kind of work that you can see, but then none of them guys do. He be a BC Indian of some kind, he told us once the name of his tribe but it be long and spelled funny and I forget it right away.

Mr. Paul ain't a very happy man, he be about 30 and I think he is what's called a sociologist. Anyway he went to university for about ten years so he could maybe be of some help to his people. Then the Government send him out here to work with us instead of his own tribe.

BC Indians be a lot different than Alberta Indians, only thing the same is we both be sort of owned by the Department of Indian Affairs. Our customs all be different and Mr. Paul can't hardly talk to us at all.

"Hey, Mr. Paul," my friend Frank Fence-post say. "What do you flat-face Indians do when you got a young girl want to leave the tribe and go to the city?"

Mr. Paul he don't like to be called a flat-face Indian. He is pretty short and bow-legged, got eyes real wide apart and his face look like it been hit a few times with a flat iron.

"We put them in the longhouse until they calm down," he tell us.

"What is this longhouse?" Charlie Cardinal ask him.

Well I bet it is the first time Mr. Ernest Paul is feel useful since he left his own reserve, cause he give us a talk for about an hour on the whole history of the longhouse in his tribe and how it be used to made medicine.

I wish Mad Etta, our medicine man, would of been there so she could tell us what she thinks, but she be away down to the Red Pheasant Reserve in Saskatchewan, attend a meeting of medicine men from all across the country.

The longhouse, Mr. Paul explain, be like a dance hall only for Indian ceremonies. When somebody has done something bad, or want to do something that against tribal custom, they get put in the longhouse. They is left alone in there for a few days, sometimes for a couple of weeks or more, until they be sorry for what they done and ready to make a new start. Then everybody is have a big party and dance — they call it a potlach in BC — and give gifts to the person who been in the longhouse so they can make a new start. Me and Frank, and Rufus Firstrider sure like the idea of that big party, but Charlie Cardinal like the idea of the longhouse better than anybody else cause he figures that a few days in there change the mind of Poppy Twelvetrees.

We all sit around and try to figure where we could put Poppy Twelvetrees that would be like a BC Indian longhouse. The Blue Quills Hall down to Hobbema Crossing be the first place that come to mind.

"What if we have to leave her there for quite a while?" Charlie say. "There be bingo there on Tuesdays and Thursdays and a dance every Saturday. Pretty hard to be alone at a bingo game."

We decide against use the Blue Quills Hall.

Since it be summer, Frank suggest that we break open the Reserve school and put her in there. "Couldn't be nothing worse than be locked up in a school," he say. "She change her mind about go to the city pretty fast if we was to put her in there."

Then somebody remember that Poppy

Twelvetrees like school. She only go until the day she be fifteen, but it be because her father, Harry Twelvetrees make her quit. He say girls got no business learn things out of books.

Finally, about the only thing we can think of is that there be an empty granary sit out in the field about 200 yards behind Wolfchild's cabin.

"That make one hell of a short longhouse," say Frank Fence-post when he see it.

It's true. It only be about 8 by 10, got a little peaked roof, one door and no windows. It be pretty dark, smell of grain dust and mice, and when the sun shine through the cracks in the boards it show the air full of dust. It sit up on skids about a foot or more off the ground and it sound kind of scary to walk across the hollow floor. We get busy and nail all the boards in place real good and make up a heavy bar to keep the door closed, instead of the little snib that was used for hold it shut. Inside we put two pieces of tree trunk, one big and one little to be a chair and a table. No need for a bed, Mr. Paul say, cause the person in there is supposed to meditate and dream things.

We arrange that we going to take turns bringing her food and water, it be between me and Frank and Rufus. We all agree that she shouldn't see Charlie until after she change her mind. The less she argue while she thinking the better, we figure. It must look kind of funny all us guys marching back and forth to that granary, sit way out there like a puddle of grey water in the green field. The field planted to oats and it be about three feet high and swirling green like pictures I seen of the ocean.

We worry some that the toilet gonna be a problem, but we borrow Louis Coyote's pickup truck that night and drive into Wetaskiwin to a spot where they building a new motel, where we borrow without asking their Johnny-on-the-Spot, which we set in the field behind the granary. Real late that night, we, as Frank Fence-post call it, put the snatch on Poppy Twelvetrees.

She don't put up no big fight cause she know us all and know we not going to hurt her. She sure do get mad though when we empty out the pockets of her jeans.

"You guys ain't even gonna leave me no cigarettes or lipstick?" she say.

"Can't," we tell her. "Can't have no white man stuff around an Indian longhouse."

We wait around outside for a while to see if she be okay. We hear her cry some, bang on the walls and kick at the door. But we nailed the place up good and she can't break it open. I can tell her crying is from be mad at us not from be scared, so we all go home.

"You changed your mind yet, Poppy?" I ask her the next night when I bring her a bologna sandwich and a jam pail full of hot chocolate that sure do burn my hands when I carry it.

"No way I gonna change my mind."

"Well it only be one day. Mr Paul say sometimes it take a couple of weeks or more."

"You can leave me here until the snow comes. Maybe if I get cold enough I promise just to get out. But as soon as you let me out I move to the city."

"We can't leave you here that long, Poppy. Emmanuel Wolfchild need this here granary come harvest."

Things go pretty much the same for the next few days. We have to keep telling Charlie we think she change her mind any time, cause he sure get anxious all the time. It is about the fourth or fifth day that I begin to see that what is wrong with what we're doing is that Poppy don't have no reason to believe in what is happening. We is just try out Ernest Paul's idea. All Poppy knows about the longhouse is what we told her while we is driving her down here in Louis Coyote's pickup, and we probably got it pretty confused by then. It don't be a holy place to Poppy, like it would be to one of Ernest Paul's Indians. Poppy don't be the kind of girl who believe in commune with no spirits. You got to be taught that stuff from a kid.

About the fifth day Poppy is say to me, "Why don't you talk serious with me, Silas? You're the smart one of that bunch. If anybody come close to understand why I want to leave it be you. Not one person has listened to me yet, least of all Charlie."

I think about Poppy all the next day and decide that I'm going to listen to her when I bring her supper. I bring her some raisin buns from the store at Hobbema. I open up the door of the granary and we sit in the doorway look at the sunset and smell the sweet green of the oats. I brought along a couple of Cokes and I give Poppy a cigarette.

"You know it be because we your friends that we do this to you," I tell her.

She nod her head.

"You sure you don't change your mind even a little bit? You don't have to marry Charlie right now, and maybe you could just move to Wetaskiwin instead of Edmonton. Sort of work yourself away a few miles at a time."

"Being here in this longhouse, as you call it, did make me think some, but it make me want all the more to leave, Silas. All I can see ahead of me is houses with not enough windows, oil-drum stoves and babies that are cough and be cold all the time. Them is the things I think about here and been think about for a long time."

"Not everybody live that way anymore." But she go on like she hardly even hear me.

"You know how sometimes, to be funny, we play a record faster than it should be? That's the way I want my life to be. I want to dance fast even to slow music. I heard what happen to some of the girls who go to the city but I think it be worse to keep on staying here and not live at all."

"If I marry Charlie, I just going to sit here and have babies, and pretty soon I be too old and too fat and ugly to even dance at all. Charlie probably never gonna build that cabin that he talk about. If I marry him we end up live in with his folks. Charlie he can go away and ride in the rodeos, or he can go to town and get drunked up, but I just sit at home and know that when he come back, maybe he love me or maybe he beat on me. I be what everybody say is a good woman, take my troubles and be quiet, like your Ma was for so many years until Paul Ermineskin left her, or like Annie Bottle is now."

"You gonna get old in the city, too, you know."

"Some Indian girls make it in the city, Silas. Your sister married with a white man. Maybe I do too, but even if I don't, even if I just get drunk a lot and die pretty soon, I gonna dance a lot before I die. Silas, if I stay here I'm already dead."

"How you gonna look after yourself? Have you thought about it at all?"

"I got $50 I saved from work at the concession at the arena. I get me a room someplace, try to get a job wait on tables. Silas, one time when we was up to Edmonton I seen a girl in the beer parlour at the Royal Hotel, she was an Indian girl, and she have some yellow flowers in her hair, and she be real happy. She wave to everybody who come into the bar and they all wave back and smile at her. Her table got, I bet, twenty glasses of beer on it, and there be people come and go all the time, laugh and make a party. I'm gonna be like her, Silas. It doesn't matter to me if it not be for very long."

When Rufus Firstrider come to give Poppy her breakfast she be gone. There be a couple of boards broke out from the back wall. He say they was ones that was nailed real good and she sure must have got strong to bust them out herself.

She ain't nowhere around the reserve. Her little brother say she sneaked in real late and took away some clothes and nail polish and stuff. Charlie Cardinal take the bus up to Edmonton and look around all day, but he don't find her. Mr. Ernest Paul walk around with his head down and don't hardly talk to anybody.

What I figure happen is that somebody help her break out those couple of boards from the wall. Then somebody maybe took Louis Coyote's pickup and drove her up to Edmonton, or maybe they drove her down to Ponoka and put her on the southbound midnight bus. That's what I figure. Other people can think what they like.

Gooch

"I heard there was Indians here," he said. He is look around the inside of the pool hall at Hobbema Crossing and try and get his eyes used to the dark after come in from the sunlight.

We just heard the south-going bus stop outside on the gravel, and we guess that is where he come from.

"There is about two thousand Indians live around here," say Robert Coyote, who is lining up the pink ball on the table next to ours.

"Then I guess there be room for one more," the new guy says. "They call me Gooch." And he hold out his hand to me, cause I am the closest Indian to the door.

"Silas," I say. He got a grip like a muskrat trap. "This here's Robert and Eathen," I point to the two guys playing snooker. "And these is Paul Cutknife, Sandra Coyote, and Sadie Onewound," I point out the three people play on the same table with me.

Gooch, he ain't shy with strangers like most

Indians, but he ain't pushy either. He just act like he been one of us all his life, and he is the kind of person can get away with do something like that.

Gooch is tall and lean and his muscles bulge like links of logging chain. His hair is long and wild, his eyes wide apart. His bottom lip been split pretty bad, from a fight I'd guess, and he got big gaps in his face where he lost some teeth someplace. He be a mean-looking Indian until he is smile, then it is like parts of his face move around change places with each other and it is just like when the sun come up in the morning.

He got big, rough hands, and tattoos on both his arms. A snake and knife on one, a motorcycle on the other, say 'Lone Wolf,' underneath in red ink.

"I'm a Tlingit Indian come all the way from Alaska," he tells us.

"So what?" say Paul Cutknife, who don't like the way his girlfriend, Sandra Coyote is looking at this strange dude.

This sort of surprise us cause Paul he usually don't have much to say to anybody. He been Sandra's boyfriend for a year or so. He is spend most of his time up on the side of the hill above our cabins, carve totems from big trees he cut down. He even sold one to the Sundance Retirement Home in Wetaskiwin. Paul is small and slim built, he got black-rimmed glasses and his ears stand out from his head some. Him and

Sandra ain't promised or nothing, I don't even know if they sleep together when they get the chance.

"Hey, Partner, I don't mean you no harm," Gooch says to Paul. "Last thing I want is trouble. I just got out of the joint down to Fort Saskatchewan. Ninety days for possession of stolen property." He laugh some and it is a nice friendly laugh. "I was walking down the street in Edmonton carrying this here TV set I'd just liberated from a motel room, when the cops come along. It was 2.30 in the morning. Even I get myself in some spots I can't talk my way out of."

"I done time, too," Robert Coyote says, and they talk some about that. I look over at Paul and he is hold his face so tight I can hardly see where his mouth should be.

Gooch never stop talking and pretty soon everybody is laugh a lot at some of his stories. He pays for our pool games, buys Cokes for us all and cigarettes for the girls. Sandra Coyote misses all her shots cause she is never take her eyes off Gooch's face.

"Gooch means wolf in my language," he says, looking right back at Sandra. "That's me a lone wolf, alright."

He is wearing jeans with a wide leather belt that got a silver buckle with a pale blue stone of some kind about two inches square set in it. He got a denim vest and a purple cowboy shirt with the sleeves rolled up, and open most to his waist. And his boots, boy, they is the fanciest pair I ever seen, hand-tooled with silver toe-caps, must of cost $200.

"A guy like me needs a good pair of boots," he say, after I tell him how much I like them. "Sometimes I got a lot of kicking to do. And sometimes, too, they is about all I got to be proud of, that and just being – a man. That's what my Old Man always used to tell me. He got drunk and walked off a pier one night; found him floating like a rat in a well the next morning. I never go looking for trouble but it sure seem to come looking for me."

We all go over to the café and Gooch buys us hamburgers and stuff. Only Paul Cutknife insist on buy his own. Paul been trying to get Sandra to leave all afternoon.

Sandra is good looking. She been most of the way through high school too. She got long dark hair kind of combed down across one eye, her nose is straight and her eyes big and black. She look like maybe she be related to some of them Indian chiefs I got in a picture book from the Westaskiwin library. She is wearing a red blouse under her jean jacket that show her nice breasts, and her blue jeans is tight enough to make guys look over their shoulder at her.

Gooch, he tell stories on himself. He don't brag about all the things he done, yet I bet he could if he wanted to. I like him.

"First time I shipped out from Alaska on a freight boat to Seattle I was maybe sixteen, and I don't speak no English at all, only Tlingit. By the time I get to Seattle all I know how to say is yes and no. A bunch of us is sitting in a bar in Seattle when this big guy come up and yell something at me. I figure I don't want no trouble so I better agree with him, so I say yes. Well that big bugger knocks me off my chair and puts the boots to me, couple of guys pull him off or he like to have killed me. What he'd said to me was 'Anybody here looking for a fight?' and I'd said, yes.

"That ain't all though. Next time we were in the bar the same guy comes up and yells at me again. I sure don't want him after me again so I say, no. Well he knocks me down again and I have to be rescued again. What he'd said was, 'Didn't you get enough of a beating last time?' I made up my mind right then that I was going to learn to speak English real good."

He tell lots more stories too, about work in the lumber camps in Washington, being in jail in Alaska, and how his white foreman's wife chased after him when he work on a ranch in the Cariboo.

"You guys figure I can get a place to stay around here? I got money," and he tap the back pocket of his jeans. "I had a few bucks when I was arrested, and what with me being American and all, they was supposed to deport me for being a crook. I talked them into a one-way ticket to Fairbanks. They trusted me to go. I cashed in the ticket in Edmonton and here I am."

I been figuring that we could put him up at our place and Ma could sure use the money.

"There's lots of room at our place," say Sandra Coyote. "Robert's going on the rodeo tomorrow and you can have his bed."

Paul Cutknife stomp out, slam the door make the plates jump on the table.

"Maybe it be better if I go with Silas," Gooch say to Sandra. "I don't want to make no trouble for you." He got his hand on her shoulder when he say this, and I can practically see Sandra Coyote's knees wobbling while she is talking to him.

"We ain't married or nothing," says Sandra.

It seems funny to me that none of us guys is mad at Gooch for the way he moves in and makes himself at home. Some people got a special way about them and he is one of those.

"I must be getting old," say Gooch. "Another time when that little guy gave me the evil eye, I'd of wiped the floor with him and then looked around to see who minded. I was trying to stay out of a fight back there."

Robert Coyote likes Gooch too, and if Robert says something is okay then the rest of us think so too. Robert is strong and mean, rides in the rodeos, been in jail, and he is also

Sandra's big brother. "If she wants to be Gooch's woman, that's her business, not mine. I wish her luck," says Robert as we walk up the hill from town to our cabins.

I try to figure how I might feel if it been my girlfriend Sadie that is get all hot for Gooch. I would sure feel bad but I don't think I make any trouble. I don't think you can make somebody love you with your fists or a gun.

A week or so later, Gooch, he went into Wetaskiwin, got himself a job first try, run a road grader for the Department of Highways.

"You got to be confident," he tells us guys that night. "First time I ever got a construction job I just walked into a camp in Alaska, told them I was the best goddamned heavy equipment operator they ever laid eyes on.

"I couldn't even find the ignition on the machine they gave me but I got to mess with it for three hours before they ran me off. Next camp I lasted a whole day, until I couldn't find the brake and drove a cat into a gravel pit full of water. But I learned. Now, when I tell them I'm the best I ain't lying no more."

One Saturday night we borrow Louis Coyote's pickup truck so a bunch of us can go to town drink beer for a while, then go to the dance at Blue Quills Hall at Hobbema.

"How about if I drive?" say Gooch. "I used to race stock cars down in Washington."

"You got a driver's license?"

"What kind would you like?" and he pull out a whole wallet full of cards. "I got Alberta, BC, Washington, Alaska and North West Territories. Name's a little different on each one. If I go to the city I draw welfare on some of them, and unemployment on my own name, if I can get it. When you live by your wits like I do, you take everything that you can get." He stops and laughs that big long laugh of his. "Got caught once. Four months for fraud. Was supposed to be deported that time too."

At the dance at Blue Quills, Paul Cutknife is pretty drunk and stagger around the hall, which ain't usual for him. In fact I never know Paul to drink hardly at all.

"You took my woman," he say, and swing his fist at Gooch. Gooch knocks him right across the hall with a couple of punches. Some farmers on the other side, stand Paul up and push him right back at Gooch, who is shove him down on the floor out of the way, cause by now there is a real good fight starting. Frank Fence-post done a little war dance and hit one of the fat farmers that picked up Paul. Pretty soon everybody is push and shove some. Frank get up on the little bench that run along the side of the hall. "Let's take us some scalps," he yell and jump right in the middle of everybody.

Boy, it is the best fight we had in a long time. Gooch and Eathen Firstrider toss farmers all over the hall until the RCMP guys is come.

Then everybody gets quiet and start to dance some, and except for a little blood on the floor and a few spots up the wall, nobody ever know there been a fight at all.

Everyone is surprised when Gooch, he keep his job for maybe three months, cause he been tell us how he one time had twenty jobs in one year and how he never stay in one place for more than a few weeks.

"This ain't a bad place, Silas," he say to me one day. "I been thinking about settling down here. I been on the road for nine years now, running from place to place like the wolf I'm named for. Sandra's a good woman and I like maybe to get us a place of our own. Guess not being a Cree I couldn't build here on your reserve, but maybe we get a place in Wetaskiwin, or maybe right here in Hobbema. The people here are pretty good, Silas. I make me some friends. There is only Paul Cutknife get all hot and bothered about me. Usually it is the other way about. I maybe got one friend and everybody else is want me to go."

I wish sometimes that I could fight like Gooch, but I don't really mind that I can't. What I do wish is that maybe I could dance like him. I'm watch him dance one night at Blue Quills with my Sadie One-wound, and I say to Sandra, "That Gooch is some dancer."

"Girls can tell a lot about a guy by dance with him," Sandra say to me. "Some guys, even if they smart or got big cars, they make a girl feel uncomfortable because they ain't sure of themselves. When I dance with Gooch I just relax, I don't have to think, all I have to do is dance because Gooch knows exactly what he's doing. And it the same with everything about him, Silas." And she give me the prettiest smile.

Nothing's a secret for very long on the reserve. Pretty soon everybody is know that Gooch and Sandra going to get their own place. Maybe even get married some people say.

Paul Cutknife hardly come out of his cabin for quite a few days.

Gooch he walks rough and laughing. His joy is to be alive. He walk through the little rooms of our cabins like he was still outside. And like my Ma say, "When Gooch is around you know there is a man in the house."

One evening Gooch, he takes Louis Coyote's pickup to town to buy groceries at the Safeway store. About 11.00 there is a little knock at my door and Gooch slip inside.

"I'm in some trouble, Silas. Paul Cutknife went to the RCMP told them about how I supposed to be deported. They pulled me over on the highway a while ago and they got a warrant for me. I shouldn't of, I know, but I blew up. I cold-cocked one of them Mounties, and split into the bush while the other one was shooting at me. I walked back to the equipment yard and hot-wired one of the Department of Highways' pickups. I got it stashed in the bush at the foot of the hill. If the Mounties ain't been here already they will be soon. I want you to go over to Coyote's and get Sandra. If we can get to Calgary they won't find us for a while."

Just as I'm about to go out the door, he puts his hand on my arm, and that mean face of his break up in a smile.

"I thought it was going to be okay here, but guess trouble follow me like a can tied to my tail."

I go over to Coyote's cabin. I tell Sandra that Gooch is wait for her at my place. Paul is there. I guess he must of told Sandra what he done.

"The Mounties gonna get him, Sandra. Stay with me," says Paul.

Sandra is wrapping up a few of her clothes in a white shirt she wear sometimes tied in a bow across her belly. She don't answer him.

"He ain't no good. He get drunk lots. He be mean to you."

"You went for him at the dance," say Sandra.

"I never been drunk before, or since. I figured if I could fight him you might...."

"I got to go."

"He'll leave you first chance."

"Maybe."

"You'll be sorry if you go."

"We made a baby, Gooch and me."

Paul Cutknife's face sort of break up like a cup been dropped on the floor. He run out of the cabin, leave the door hanging open. I don't know what he going to do but I sure hurry Sandra over to our place. I don't know if I imagine it or not but I think I can see where her belly bulge a little bit over the top of her jeans.

"I'm sorry, Babe," Gooch says. "If you don't want to go I understand."

"You're in trouble because of me. I don't quit you now."

I only got twenty dollars or so but I hand it to Gooch.

Sandra draw in her breath real sharp, and there is Paul in the doorway. He is coming for Gooch and the big blade of his carving knife is shine in the lamplight. They circle each other a bit.

My brother Hiram runs up to the door. "Cops is coming," he say.

"I'm gonna kill you," say Paul Cutknife. "You be dead by the time the Mounties get here."

"Make your move," say Gooch.

Paul has his back mostly to me as I take a plate off the table and smash it on the floor. Paul turns to look at the noise and Gooch has him. He trip his feet out from under him and they roll a couple of times on the floor. Gooch bites into Paul's arm as he pushes his knife hand down and the knife comes free. Gooch pushes it over to me and I put it in my belt.

"Get out!" Gooch says to Paul as he lets him up. Gooch never hurt him except to do what he had to, to get the knife from him. I wonder if I be so easy on him if he turned me into the RCMP and tried to kill me. Paul runs out the door and across the clearing, holding on to the arm that been bit.

The RCMP car is almost up to the cabins.

"Help me any way you can, Silas," Gooch says as he and Sandra disappear around the side of the cabin.

I go out and act real scared for the RCMP.

"If you guys looking for Gooch," I say, "he's over to Coyote's cabin. But be real careful he's got a couple of rifles."

They shut off all their lights quick and go sneak off in the dark toward Coyote's cabin. I take Paul's knife and first cut off the cord to their radio microphone, then poke holes in both front tires.

I hear the pickup roar from down at the foot of the hill and away it goes on the road to Hobbema. I start to breathe easy.

Then from high up in the trees, up where Paul Cutknife does his carving, come rifle shots. In the dark I can see the little scarlet flashes, like a snake flick his tongue.

The pickup goes down off the left side of the road, travel in the ditch for a while, then come back up and across, and end up pointing down at the slough.

I can hear the RCMP guys' boots on the gravel as they run up toward the rifle fire. The shots just keep coming and coming, little red flashes are close together and I can hear the bullets keep crash into the truck. The headlights make funny colours on the slough water like the Northern Lights do sometimes in the sky.